For a few moments we just sat in the car, not talking. All my life, when things had gone wrong, I'd always looked for a way to make them right again. If I said the wrong thing, I apologized, or if I broke something, I tried to fix it, or if someone else had a problem, I tried to help them. But what could I do for Howie? There was only one thing that could make things right again, and that was curing him. But no one knew if that could be done.

TODD STRASSER'S writing has appeared in many publications including *The New Yorker* and *The Village Voice*. His successful first novel, *Angel Dust Blues,* is also available in a Laurel-Leaf edition. Mr. Strasser lives in New York City.

FRIENDS TILL THE END

Todd Strasser

LAUREL-LEAF BOOKS bring together under a single imprint outstanding works of fiction and nonfiction particularly suitable for young adult readers, both in and out of the classroom. Charles F. Reasoner, Professor Emeritus of Children's Literature and Reading, New York University, is consultant to the series.

Published by
Dell Publishing
a division of
Bantam Doubleday Dell Publishing Group, Inc.
666 Fifth Avenue
New York, New York 10103

To Ken, Gladys, and Judy
And to the memory of Jed

The trademark Laurel-Leaf Library® is registered in the U.S. Patent
and Trademark Office.

ISBN: 0-440-92625-4

RL: 6.2

Reprinted by arrangement with Delacorte Press
Printed in the United States of America

April 1982

10 9 8

KRI

CHAPTER ONE

The villages of Cooper's Neck and Cooper's Point are located on the North Shore of Long Island, in an area nicknamed the Gold Coast. The name goes back to the early 1900s, when wealthy families like the Whitneys and Vanderbilts lived here. But they're gone now, and all that's left of their magnificent estates are one- and two-acre lots complete with ranch houses, cesspool problems, and crabgrass.

The funny thing is, people around here still act like real snobs about the Gold Coast. Listening to them, you'd think it was the greatest place in the world to live. Who knows? Maybe they're right. At least, every time a piece of land goes up for sale and a new development is built, the houses never stay vacant for long. Outsiders do seem eager to move in. But, if you ask me, I think they're just suckers for a fancy address.

My father says the only difference between Cooper's Neck and anyplace else is that things cost more here. He's a real estate agent and he's always saying that if it wasn't for the business, he'd move to someplace like Maine. But meanwhile he's making pretty good bucks staying here.

Sometimes, though, even he gets disgusted. Like, when they named the new development down the street from us Cooper's Neck Estates, even though each "estate" was only half an acre large and you could still see the stripes in the lawns where the sod had been laid. My father said the new houses were "orange crates" and he expected a few to blow away with the first strong wind. Of course, that didn't stop him from selling them. Ask him why and he'll tell you he can't make a living turning people away.

The Jamisons were the first family to move into Cooper's Neck Estates. They came from Florida; Mr. Jamison's company transferred him to their New York office. I knew this because Howie Jamison told me. Howie was a senior, like me, and I met him at the bus stop on the first morning of school. His hair fell straight down on his forehead and over his ears a little, reminding me of the Beatles on their early albums. He wore green plaid pants, white loafers with tassles, and a baggy yellow cardigan sweater, and I had to restrain myself from asking where his golf clubs were. Nobody at

Cooper's Neck High wore clothes like that. This guy has got to be weird, I thought.

But the funny thing was, I sort of liked Howie Jamison. At the bus stop he always acted like he was glad to see me. And he wasn't embarrassed to admit that he was new and lonely and trying to make friends. You could see that he was kind of perplexed about moving north. Like, he told me that in Florida his family had lived on a canal called the Inter-coastal and he had his own little twelve-foot racing boat. When he heard he was moving to Long Island he figured he'd bring his boat, but he got up here and found the island was so big he still wasn't sure where the water was. He also had a small motorcycle he used to drive in Florida, where the driving age is fourteen, but it was sitting in his new garage in Cooper's Neck Estates because the driving age on Long Island is seventeen, if you've taken driver's ed. In a way he was lost, a jockey without his horse. "I mean," he said on the second morning of school, "what *does* a body do up here?" He also talked a little funny.

I told him that bodies around Cooper's Neck played sports, saw movies, hung around town or went to the city. Bodies used to cruise in their cars, but with the price of gas, no one could afford it anymore.

"You got an Optimists Club?" he asked.

"A what?"

Howie looked at me in disbelief. "You know, a club or service organization. Like the Lions or the Jaycees. How do you get a softball game organized or a picnic or a dance?"

I told him I hadn't been to a dance or a picnic since the eighth grade and that if you wanted to play softball, you just called up a bunch of guys and played.

Howie shook his head wonderingly. "It sure is different up here," he said.

As far as I could tell, Howie was the one who was different, but he was also, well, refreshing in a way. True, he seemed younger and more naive than other guys my age, and he did dress funny, but he also got excited and interested about things and didn't pretend to always be cool like your typical Gold Coaster. I'd get down to the bus stop each morning, grumpy and still aching from the previous evening's soccer practice, and Howie would be waiting there, full of news about his most recent adventure.

"I found a Carvel!" he announced on the third morning, as if he'd just won the million-dollar lottery or something.

"So?"

"Like the one I worked at in Florida," he explained. "I talked to the owner and he said he might be able to use me on weekends." He slapped his hands together. "Boy, I didn't think there'd be one in Cooper's Neck."

"Howie, I know it's different here, but it's **not** a foreign country."

Howie laughed. "Could've fooled me."

Not only did Howie come down to the bus stop each morning dressed like he was going out to play eighteen holes in the Bob Hope Golf Classic, but he carried his books in one of those thick rubber bands we'd used in grade school. The rest of us carried our books in nylon day packs. On the fourth morning he also brought a trumpet case and told me he wanted to join the school band.

"I don't think we have a band, Howie," I said.

"Come on, every school has a band," he said. "You know, to play at football half times and stuff."

I laughed. "I hate to tell you this, but the Cooper's Neck football team hasn't won a game in two years. Nobody does anything at half time because hardly anyone goes to the games."

Howie shrugged. "Well, I'm not crazy about band music anyway. I like jazz, you know? Like Miles Davis and Maynard Ferguson."

I gave him a blank look and he said, "Come on, David, you must have heard of Maynard Ferguson."

The next thing I knew, Howie put down the case and took out the trumpet. He stuck the mouthpiece in and fingered the valves, and I realized he was going to play it right there at the bus stop. "I wouldn't . . ." I started to say, but it was too late.

There must have been about a dozen kids stand-

5

ing around the bus stop and when Howie hit the first note, they all turned and stared at him. The first few notes he played weren't bad, but then he hit this incredibly high, screeching wail and held it for about twenty seconds.

The kids just about went berserk. "Hey, cut it out!" "What're you doing?" "It's seven-thirty in the morning, you jerk!"

Howie pulled the trumpet from his lips. His face was red and he was panting. "That's Maynard Ferguson's trademark," he told the angry little crowd.

"Yeah? Well, shove it," someone said.

Howie looked dismayed, as if he couldn't understand why they were so rude to him. He quickly put the instrument away and gave me a quizzical look. I was just taking my fingers out of my ears.

"Some of these kids just woke up, Howie," I said.

He nodded. "You sure you never heard of Maynard Ferguson?" he asked one last time.

It was obvious that Howie wanted us to be good friends, and I found myself in an awkward position. I already had a close group of friends, most of them on the soccer team, and I had a soccer practice every afternoon. At night there was homework. Since the spring before, I'd been thinking about going to medical school after college. I didn't tell any of my friends—they would have said I was crazy—but for senior year I'd signed up for an extra science course and I was studying hard. I really needed to do well that semester because I'd messed around junior year and my average was a measly two point seven. And except for another practice on Saturday mornings and the time I had to take for studying, I spent my weekends with my girl friend, Rena. That didn't leave much time for Howie, especially since he wasn't into sports, and I doubted Rena would be interested in having him along on dates.

Toward the end of the fourth day of school there was a senior assembly. I walked into the auditorium and saw Howie sitting alone. He waved for me to join him, but I'd already told Rena I'd sit with her and her friend Sara, who led one of the tightest, snobbiest cliques in school. I could have asked Howie to join us, but I knew Sara would take one look at his plaid pants and white loafers and turn on the deep-freeze treatment. Maybe I should have told Rena I was going to sit with Howie, but I didn't. Instead I just waved back to Howie and left him sitting alone.

I felt bad about that, but in a way I also hoped that Howie would get the message: it wasn't that I didn't like him, but I just didn't have the time in my life for a new friend. Unfortunately, he didn't get it. In fact, on the bus to school the next morning he wanted to know if I'd come over to his house that night for dinner.

"Shouldn't you ask your mother first?" I said,

looking for an excuse. It sounded so corny, like inviting someone to sleep over. Besides, who wanted to have friends over to dinner with their parents? It was bad enough that *you* had to eat with your parents.

"She'd love it," Howie said. "She likes company."

"Well, maybe another time," I said. "I got a lot of homework tonight."

Howie was quiet for a moment and then he nodded slowly. "Yeah, sure," he said.

It wasn't until we got off the bus that I realized it was the fifth morning of the week, Friday. Nobody did homework on Friday night.

The following Monday morning Howie wasn't at the bus stop. He didn't show up Tuesday, Wednesday, or the rest of the week either. A lot of seniors at Cooper's Neck had cars and drove to school, and I figured Howie had probably made friends with someone and was getting a ride every morning. In a way I felt relieved. It was a big enough school, about three hundred kids per grade, and I was glad that Howie had found some new friends. Hopefully they were into the things Howie was into. Maybe they'd even know who Maynard Ferguson was.

CHAPTER TWO

About two weeks later I learned that Howie was in the hospital. My parents and I were just sitting down to dinner one night when the phone rang. None of us wanted to get up and answer it.

"It's business," my mother told my father.

"It's one of your friends," my father told me.

"It's Aunt Brenda," I told my mother.

The phone rang again. My mother sighed and got up. She was the only one in the family who couldn't let a phone call go unanswered. Meanwhile, my father started serving the pot roast. "Any new invitations?" he asked, referring to the colleges and universities that wanted me to visit their campuses and accept an athletic scholarship in return for four years of goaltending.

"Nope," I said. My father didn't know that I, David Gilbert, soon to be six-year veteran goalie of Cooper's Neck High's outstanding soccer team, did not think I would be accepting an athletic scholarship to college next year. Nor did he suspect that I was seriously considering pursuing a pre-med education at an approximate cost of $30,000 for four years on an undergraduate level, not to mention med school. I had not yet informed my father of this because, frankly, I did not want to start a Gilbert family equivalent of World War III.

"What schools have invited you so far?" he asked.

"Hartwick, Temple, and C. W. Post."

He smiled. "And any one of them could offer you a scholarship?"

"What if I decide to go to a school that doesn't give scholarships?" I asked. That summer I'd taken courses in biology and psychology and had gotten an A and A– respectively. They were the first A's of my life (other than gym), but I still hadn't told my parents about my new plans. They thought I'd gone to summer school to avoid getting some crummy summer job.

My father picked a piece of food from between his teeth and frowned. "What kind of soccer team could they have if they don't give scholarships?"

Fortunately, my mother returned to the table before I had to explain. She sat down, but didn't start eating. "That was Elizabeth Jamison," she said. "Howard Jamison's mother. Did you know that he was in the hospital?"

"No," I said, surprised. I hadn't thought about Howie in days.

"He has leukemia," my mother said.

"Who's this?" my father asked.

"Remember that couple from Florida?" my mother said. "You sold them their house. The white one, third on the left as you drive into the new development."

My father thought about it for a second. "Oh, yes. He's an accountant. Nice people." Anyone who bought a house from my father was automatically "nice people."

My mother turned back to me. "Mrs. Jamison said you and Howard became friends before he became ill."

"We did?"

"She said he often spoke of you."

"Oh . . . I didn't know."

"She wanted to know if you would go see him in the hospital," my mother said. "He asked for you."

"I've got soccer practice," I said. Our first match was only a week away.

"Can't you skip a day?" she asked.

"Go after practice," my father said.

I didn't know what to say.

"They're new here, David," my mother said. "Howard must be lonely . . ."

In the goal sometimes you get hit by so many

shots so fast you don't have time to prepare for each one. Instead, you just react instinctively. Now my mother was hitting me so fast my instincts took over and said, "*I hardly know the guy, how come I have to visit him?*"

"Do I have to?" I asked.

I felt my mother's eyes lock on me. "David, do you know what it means to have leukemia?"

I didn't know specifically, but I had a feeling. "He's really sick, huh?"

My mother nodded.

"Could I catch it?" I asked.

My mother and father looked at each other for a moment. Then she said, "I don't think it's contagious, David. You'll go tomorrow, won't you?"

"Let me think about it," I said.

That night I had trouble concentrating on my homework. My thoughts kept slipping from the textbook in front of me to Howie. He hadn't been at the bus stop in almost two weeks. I had noticed at first, but then I'd been so busy. . . .

Actually, even that first week I'd hardly seen him during the day in school. We had different classes and lunch periods and I always stayed after school for soccer practice. It wasn't surprising that I assumed he was getting a ride from someone when he stopped showing up at the bus stop. Still, it didn't seem right that I'd just forgotten about him.

There were two light raps on my door, my mother's knock. "Can I come in?"

"Sure."

She sat down on my bed, her hands clasped and pressed into her lap. I was familiar with that pose; it was the one she used with my father when she asked for compassion, understanding, or money for new clothes. My mother was definitely the humanitarian of the family. She taught school, marched with the ASPCA against cruel animal experimentation, raised funds for Cambodian refugees, and once drove all the way to Philadelphia to give blood for a woman in the teachers' union. "If Howard has no other friends, David, it's important that you go see him," she said.

I didn't answer right away. Inside I felt divided. On one hand I knew my mother was right. It had been wrong for me to just stop thinking about Howie in the first place and this was an opportunity to make amends. And it was important because he was really sick. But on the other hand I didn't see why the responsibility for comforting him should fall on me, a veritable stranger, just because I'd talked to him at the bus stop. "You know," I said, "we really aren't friends. We just took the bus to school a couple of times."

13

My mother nodded. I suspected she'd known that all along. "It doesn't matter now whether you are friends or not," she said. "He's alone, and he doesn't know anyone else his own age. Can you put yourself in his position?"

I could. She was right. I said I'd go.

CHAPTER
THREE

Before soccer practice the next day I looked for Rena in the school darkroom. That was where you could find her any time she didn't have a class or a yearbook or newspaper meeting. A lot of students shared the darkroom and sometimes when you walked in, it was so dark you couldn't tell who was in there. But when Rena was working, the darkroom was always filled with cigarette smoke.

"Where are you?" I asked. The room was totally dark and so smoky I knew only Rena could be in there. Sometimes I thought she purposely smoked in the darkroom just to keep other photographers out.

"At the developing trays," she answered. "Don't move until I turn on the safelight, okay?"

"Okay." I stood in the dark, listening to the clink of metal tongs on trays and the sloshing of solutions as Rena worked, meanwhile rehearsing in my head the reasons why I had to break our dinner date. Rena and I usually went out for dinner on the nights when her mother, who was divorced, went to the city on a date, or stayed out overnight at a "friend's." Since Rena didn't like to cook, Mrs. Steuben always left her money for dinner.

I had to tell Rena I couldn't have dinner with her because I was going to the hospital. Actually, the more I thought about it, the more I wanted to see Howie. I knew nothing about leukemia or its treatment, and this seemed like an opportunity to learn. And I wanted Howie to know that people were concerned.

Rena would probably be pissed.

The safelight went on and the room filled with a soft red glow. In the solitude of the darkroom Rena and I kissed and I tasted cigarettes on her lips.

"I can't make it for dinner tonight," I said. "My parents asked me to go see this kid who's sick. He's the son of a friend of theirs."

"What's wrong with him?" Rena asked.

"My mother says he has leukemia."

"Oh." Rena stepped back to the developing trays.

"Actually, he just moved here this year," I said. "I used to see him at the bus stop. But I think he was only in school for about a week before he got sick. He might have been in a couple of your classes."

Rena lit a new cigarette and exhaled red-tinted smoke into the safelight. "I don't remember anyone new. What was his name?"

"Howie Jamison."

Rena thought for a moment and shook her head.

"Well, I hope you're not mad," I said.

Across the table from me Rena stirred a solution in a tray with a pair of tongs. "No, I understand," she said. "Stay still for a moment." There was a click and we went into total darkness.

Rena and I had met about a year before. The soccer team had just made it to the Class A sectionals, and suddenly soccer was big news. I'd been playing on teams at the high school since seventh grade, but I couldn't remember us ever drawing a crowd of more than thirty fans. But the day we won our section, more than two hundred spectators came, and that was when I noticed Rena Steuben taking pictures of me.

The next day I found myself in the darkroom with her. Like a lot of guys at Cooper's Neck High I'd occasionally thought about asking Rena out, but never considered it seriously. She was part of the "sophisticated" newspaper-yearbook crowd—pretty, smart (some would say snobby), always dressed well, the kind who went to the city to see a new movie instead of waiting for it to come to the local theater. I was just a jock. That meant we had different friends, different classes, different ideas. A jock and a smarty dating was Cooper's Neck High's version of a mixed couple.

The first thing she did that day in the darkroom was give me a hard time about why I didn't wear a uniform like the rest of the team. I started to explain that the rules say goalies have to wear contrasting clothes, but she pointed to a bunch of black-and-white photos spread out on a table near us.

I remember looking at the pictures and being surprised. In each one Rena had caught the peak moment, that split second between a shot and a save when you were never sure what the outcome would be. And the pictures were in focus too, a skill the photographer for the local paper had yet to master. "These are really good," I said.

Ignoring my compliment, Rena picked up one of the pictures. "At least here they'll see Chunk Lowell in a uniform near you," she said. "These others just look like practice."

"Don't worry," I told her, "they'll know it was a real game."

"How?" she asked.

I pointed to a picture of me diving across the goal mouth, arms outstretched, lunging for a ball. "I never try this hard in practice."

She stared at me for a second. It was the first time our eyes really met, and I began to wonder if going out with her would be as impossible as I'd thought. I liked the way she was so intense and intelligent, but at the same time unsure and scared that I might be making fun of her. She didn't seem so unapproachable anymore.

Anyway, I wasn't dating anyone and I figured it couldn't hurt to ask if she wanted to go out sometime. The worst she could say was no. So the next day I asked. Surprise, surprise, she said yes.

The safelight came back on, and Rena started hanging up long strips of negatives to dry. In the red light her long brown hair picked up rosy highlights. She knew I was watching her. "So when are you going to the hospital?" she asked.

"After practice."

She stepped back to a developing tray, lifted a dripping photo out of it, and pretended to scrutinize it. But I knew she was wondering why I was still standing there in the darkroom.

"You gonna get a picture of us at Seaport on Wednesday?" I asked.

"Seaport?"

"Our first game."

"I've got a yearbook meeting," she said.

"Always nice to have your girl friend rooting

for you at the first game," I said. It must have sounded pretty feeble, but I really wanted her to come.

Across the table from me Rena smiled. "You're such a cornball, David."

"I can't help it. I was born that way. Now, how about it? I'm not asking you to wave any pompoms."

"You better not."

"Will you come?"

Rena dropped the photo back into the tray. "I thought you didn't care about soccer anymore," she said, in a slightly mocking way. "I thought you'd decided to be a doctor."

"Yeah, but I still play soccer."

"So you'll be a doctor for soccer players," she said. Ever since June, when I started summer school, she'd made fun of it. Even after I got the A's, she acted like she didn't care. The grades probably didn't impress her, she'd gotten plenty of A's in her life, but I thought it would have made her understand that I was serious.

"You won't go to the game?" I asked.

"I'll try to catch the second half," she replied. "They'll want a picture for the paper." She reached for the safelight switch. Click. We were in the dark again.

CHAPTER
FOUR

West Hill Hospital is one of the best in the state, if not the whole country. There are always stories in the local newspaper about how doctors there are pioneering new techniques or operations and about how the hospital is constructing a new wing or starting some revolutionary program. Even the nurses are prettier than at other hospitals. A big joke when teams came to play at Cooper's Neck was their players pretending to get hurt so they could go to West Hill and meet a nurse. And Coach Lavelle used to say that if we had to get hurt, he hoped we'd do it on the home field, so we could be treated at the West Hill Emergency Room.

Still, no matter how excellent an institution it is, I didn't feel any better about going. Hospitals are even more depressing than funeral homes. At least at a funeral home the people are already dead, and there's nothing you can do about bringing them back, but in hospitals they are still hanging on, even if it's by the thinnest thread. But, I told myself, if I was really serious about medical school I'd have to learn to take it.

At home after school I picked up my mother's Datsun. Around Cooper's Neck High a senior without his or her own car was a rarity, but I was one of them. Most kids got a new car or a hand-me-down as soon as they passed their road test. Not the Gilbert kids. Of course, by the time I became a senior, I didn't expect a car. After all, ours was the only family on the block that didn't hire a gardener to cut the lawn or take the cars to the car wash in town. Guess who did both chores? I could remember being in ninth grade and realizing I was the only kid around who cut his own grass. For a while the prospect of being seen pushing the lawn mower across the front lawn seemed so excruciating that I rigged a flashlight to it and mowed at night. But after decapitating three lawn sprinklers and destroying two pairs of lawn mower blades, I was given an ultimatum by my father: Either start mowing during the day, or start paying for the damage done at night. I switched to days.

At West Hill I picked up a visitor's pass and was directed to the Solomon Cohen Pavilion. Almost everything at West Hill was donated by one rich Gold Coaster or another, and there were brass plaques all over telling you who gave what. I wouldn't have been surprised if the bathrooms had them: THIS TOILET DONATED BY . . .

The elevator in the Solomon Cohen Pavilion was donated by Mr. and Mrs. Richard Fox. Before the doors on the Foxes' elevator closed, a nurse came in pushing a very old man in a wheelchair. The man was wearing a hospital gown, and there was a plastic tube running up his nose. His head was tilted back, and his eyes were closed. His hair was white, and his face was pale, wrinkled, and bony. Maybe he'd be dead soon, I thought. He looked so old it didn't bother me as much as it did to think about Howie. That old guy had lived a long time and, after all, nobody lives forever. But Howie was a young guy. Like me.

Upstairs, the door to the room that was supposed to be Howie's was open, and I walked in. There were two beds inside, but neither was occupied. I was about to go back out and check the room number again when I heard someone say my name. "David?"

I turned and saw a small woman with bleached-blond hair sitting in a chair across from the empty beds. She was wearing a light-blue pantsuit that sort of reminded me of a stewardess's uniform. "Mrs. Jamison?"

The lady nodded and smiled. She was pretty, but she looked tired. "I'm so glad you could come," she said with a southern accent. "Howie's been asking for you."

"Uh, how is he?" I asked.

"He's . . ." Mrs. Jamison began to say something, but then hesitated. "Getting treatment." She sounded weary. I looked again at the empty beds. "He'll be back soon," she said. "They just took him for a test."

I got a chair, and Mrs. Jamison filled me in on what had been happening to Howie. He had a form of leukemia called AML, and while it wasn't the worst form of the disease, it wasn't the best either. The marrow in Howie's bones wasn't producing blood cells the way it was supposed to, and Howie was in the hospital to get a series of chemotherapy treatments to make the marrow work properly again. He'd already had his first set of treatments and had gone home to rest for a week. Now he was back for his second set.

"Hopefully, when he's through with this torture he'll be in remission," Mrs. Jamison said. "But the doctors say he won't be cured unless he stays in remission for five years."

Torture? What did she mean by that, I wondered. It made me feel uneasy, not understanding what she was talking about. You didn't get tortured in hospitals. Maybe she meant the disease was torture. Anyway, she had a right to be upset. Five years seemed like an impossibly long time to wait.

Howie still wasn't back, so we talked for a while about Cooper's Neck Estates. Mrs. Jamison seemed reserved, as if she was constantly holding back her true feelings. Everything was "very nice" or "seemed lovely," but I got the feeling she was just being polite. She was actually naming the kinds of trees in her backyard when suddenly this bald person wearing a ratty yellow bathrobe and pushing something that looked like a thin metal coatrack on wheels stepped into the room. For a second I thought it was an old man, but then I realized it was a kid with no hair.

"Is Howie back?" the kid asked.

"Not yet," Mrs. Jamison said.

The boy nodded and turned around. The rack carried a plastic bag filled with clear liquid that ran down a tube and disappeared up the sleeve of his robe. "I'll be back," he said, pushing the rack away.

Shock. Mrs. Jamison started talking about trees again, but I hardly heard her. Sometimes you can hear about something for years, but it doesn't mean a thing until you actually see it for the first time. For years I'd heard stories about teenagers getting killed in car accidents or overdosing on drugs, but I'd never known anyone my own age who'd died or who'd even been seriously ill. But seeing that bald kid made me realize where I was—in a hospital with doctors and nurses in the halls and patients in the beds, and somewhere Howie Jamison was being treated for a disease that sometimes killed people.

A nurse walked through the door, followed by an

orderly pushing a stretcher. Howie was lying on it.
I could see how much thinner he'd become. There
was a needle taped to his right arm and connected
by a tube to a bag above his stretcher. The same
thing that bald kid had. I remembered that they
called it an IV. Who says you can't learn anything
from television?

"Good to see you," Howie said, holding up his
left hand to shake. For a moment I hesitated while
a little neon sign in my head flashed *"Germs!"* on
and off. It was like when I was a little kid, and my
mother told me not to touch certain things like
dead animals lying on the ground. Except Howie
wasn't dead, and leukemia wasn't contagious—it
was just a crazy reaction. I grabbed his hand and
shook it. There wasn't much strength in Howie's
grip.

Mrs. Jamison and I watched while the nurse
helped Howie slide from the stretcher to his bed
and reattached the bag of liquid to a post above
him. I wasn't sure if Mrs. Jamison saw it, but
Howie flinched when the nurse moved him. When
you play sports, you learn the signs of a guy who's
hurting but tries to hide it because he doesn't want
to be taken out of the game.

"You meet my mom?" Howie asked while the
nurse fiddled with the bag above him.

"Yeah, we've been talking," I said. The nurse

glanced at me. She was blond, a bit on the short side, and quite pretty. Maybe a little too much makeup, but par for West Hill. The tag on her uniform told me she was Ms. Kirkpatrick.

Mrs. Jamison got up and went over to her son. "Are you all right?"

"Sure, Mom." But you could see how tired he was. Even speaking seemed to be a chore. Ms. Kirkpatrick disconnected the bag of clear liquid and hooked up another bag above Howie, this one cloudy and yellowish.

"Platelets?" Howie asked her.

She nodded.

"Does he need a lot?" Mrs. Jamison asked.

Ms. Kirkpatrick began to answer, but Howie cut her off. "I need whatever I need, Mom." He seemed annoyed.

"Four units," Ms. Kirkpatrick said.

Mrs. Jamison sat down again. She looked upset. Ms. Kirkpatrick adjusted Howie's blanket. "Okay?" she asked.

"Sure," Howie said. "Why don't you come back tonight after lights-out."

Ms. Kirkpatrick ignored him.

"I bet you hear that twenty times a day," Howie said.

"At least," she said, walking out.

Mrs. Jamison watched Ms. Kirkpatrick leave

and then turned to her son. "Four units, Howie . . ." she said. "And you shouldn't talk that way to a nurse."

Howie frowned. "Mom, last time I had ten units in one day. Four isn't much."

Mrs. Jamison blinked and glanced at me. I guess she didn't want to get into an argument in front of a stranger.

"Mom?" Howie said, his voice softer now. "Why don't you go home and rest. David's gonna stay for a while, right?"

"Uh, sure." I hadn't planned to, but . . .

Mrs. Jamison looked uncertain. "You're sure you won't need me?"

"David can help if I need anything," Howie said.

"Well, all right." Mrs. Jamison said. It didn't seem to take much coaxing from Howie. I had a feeling they both needed to get away from each other for a while. Mrs. Jamison picked up her bag and jacket.

"Get Dad to take you out to dinner," Howie said.

Mrs. Jamison leaned over and kissed him on the forehead.

"Not in front of my friend, Mom," Howie said. We all laughed a little. Mrs. Jamison and I told each other how nice it was to meet, and she left. I turned back to Howie, wondering what to say.

"Do me a favor, David?" Howie asked.

"Okay."

"Help me roll over on my left side a little."

It sounded like an odd request, but I did it. Howie sighed as I slipped my hands under his shoulder and helped him over.

"Thanks, David," he said. "And thanks for coming too."

"Sure." I sat down again, still puzzled.

Lying on the bed, Howie looked at me sideways. "I hate to say it, but she's starting to drive me crazy. Every little thing has some special meaning to her. If I get four units of platelets instead of two, it means I must be getting worse. If the doctor looks at her funny, it means he's hiding something. If the nurse doesn't answer the call button right away, it means they've given up. I swear, the other night they gave me a kosher meal by mistake, and she got upset. Probably thought they were trying to convert me or something."

"Platelets have something to do with blood clotting, right?" I asked, recalling something from summer school biology class.

"Yeah," Howie said. "If I don't have enough of them, I can't stop bleeding."

Just then a youngish-looking doctor stuck his head in the door. "How are you feeling today?"

Howie waved at him. "Great," he said, "considering I have no white count."

The doctor chuckled. "When do you start treatment?"

"Tomorrow morning."

"Good luck." The doctor continued down the hall.

"I'll need it!" Howie yelled after him. He looked back at me. "I feel like I'm in a zoo. The doctors come in and poke me. The nurses feed me at feeding time. People stand in the doorway and stare. Once in a while the curtains are closed and the cage gets cleaned. Don't ever get sick, David. It's a real bummer."

I nodded solemnly. Before going into the room I'd imagined us having a pleasant little chat, avoiding any mention of the disease, pretending it was just a temporary problem that was bound to clear up. But it was obvious that Howie wasn't interested in that. He wanted someone who would listen.

We talked for a long time that evening. He explained that the white count indicated the level of white cells in his blood and that he'd been kidding when he'd said he had none, although his count was low. In the last two weeks he'd learned a lot. He said the doctors didn't always want to answer his questions about leukemia and sometimes they flatly refused, but he kept badgering them. "After all," he told me, "I'm the one who's stuck with it."

Despite how sick I suspected he was, Howie didn't complain or ask for sympathy, even when he told me that the drugs they gave him made him puke for hours. It seemed like he just needed someone who would listen and not get upset. As we talked I began to realize why Howie had wanted his mother to go away. It must have scared him when she carried on so excessively. It might have been natural to fear the worst, but Howie needed some hope too.

Still, it was even hard for *me* to stay composed at times, like when Howie told me they'd jabbed a needle into his hipbone that afternoon to draw out some marrow for tests.

"That's why I asked you to turn me over," he explained. "I'm still sore." He also told me about the spinal tap he'd had his second day in the hospital, two weeks before. They had taken a sample of fluid from his spine.

"I really screamed," he said. "So the doctor who was doing the tap got mad because I startled him, you know? He told me to keep quiet, and I told him to go to hell." Howie grinned. "I never said that to an adult before in my life. It didn't stop the pain, but it felt great."

We both laughed. You had to admire Howie. From the little I knew of him at the bus stop, I wouldn't have guessed he'd be this brave about something so frightening.

"So when do you think you'll be getting out?" I asked.

Howie was quiet for a moment, and I had the feeling I'd asked the wrong question.

Finally he said, "I get seven days of treatment and then they'll let me go home." The grin disappeared and he seemed to suddenly grow depressed. "You can't believe how bad it is, David. Seven days of pills and shots that make you puke and get constipated and feel like crap. The stuff they give me is poison, but it's the only thing that stops the leukemic cells from growing."

For the second time that night I was unable to think of words to say. Howie watched me. A smile started at one corner of his mouth, but it didn't quite make it all the way around. "I didn't mean to make it sound so heavy," he said.

"That's okay, Howie."

The smile grew larger. "Right now I don't feel so bad," he said. "In fact, I can't wait for that nurse to come back."

"You want me to go out in the hall and get her?"

Howie looked up at the bag of platelets above him. It was almost empty. "No, don't bother," he said. "She'll be back soon enough."

CHAPTER
FIVE

Chunk Lowell, worshiper of the sun, captain of
the soccer team, and my best friend, wrapped his
feet in about half a mile of adhesive tape before
every game, scrimmage, and practice. We had
lockers next to each other in the locker room, and
I must have seen him do it two hundred times since
we'd started playing together. He had just finished
his left foot when I arrived.

"Hey, partner," he said. Since sophomore year,
Chunk had been developing a cowboy persona,
complete with Stetson, boots, fringed suede jacket,
and hokey Western expressions.

"Hey."

"What's with you?" he asked.

"Nothing."

"Nothing, bull. What ails you, son?"

I looked at him, sitting on the bench, muscular

and darkly tanned beneath his thick, unruly blond hair, wearing only his jock and a half a mile of tape. The Jockstrap Cowboy. "Rena's giving me a hard time about the Seaport game. Says she might only make it for the second half."

Chunk picked up an empty tape spool and arced it across the locker room into a wastebasket. "File for divorce."

"Ha, ha."

"Anyone ever tell you you're too serious about her?" Chunk asked as he started to mummify his right foot.

"Yeah, you, about twice a week," I said, sitting down and pulling my Pumas off.

"That's right," Chunk said, slapping me on the back. "Now, when are you going to believe me?"

Probably never, I thought. The concept of being serious about a girl was as foreign to Chunk as sitting on a beach in the shade. Chunk spent every summer on Martha's Vineyard, chasing girls at night and anointing himself with strange concoctions of iodine and baby oil and sleeping on the beach all day. He always had girl friends, but his relationships with them seemed to begin and end according to the school calendar, like sports.

"What else?" Chunk asked.

"How do you know there's something else?" I said.

"Hey, listen, did Laurel know Hardy? Does Mindy know Mork? Did Einstein know Relativity?"

"Chunk, remember your aunt who died last year?" I said. She'd had some kind of cancer.

"No, I've forgotten all about her," Chunk said sarcastically.

"Didn't you once tell me something about the doctors wanting her to smoke grass? It had something to do with the treatment she was getting."

"Yeah, they say if you smoke dope the side effects from the chemotherapy aren't as bad. Otherwise you puke your guts out. But she never did it. She had other problems. Like her head wasn't on right. Why do you want to know?"

"I know this guy who has leukemia, and he's been having a pretty hard time with the drugs they're giving him."

"Anyone I know?"

"No, he was only in school for the first week, then he got sick."

Chunk finished taping his right foot and stood up and bounced up and down on the balls of his feet. "Might as well tell him about it," he said. "It can't hurt."

We got into our soccer clothes and went out to the field. It was sunny, and there was still some time before practice began, so Chunk pulled off his T-shirt and positioned himself against the bench for a few minutes of tan maintenance.

"What're you going to do in the winter?" I asked.

"There's a Tan-o-rama place on Northern Boulevard," he said. "I've already started hitting it a couple of times a week. Should tide me over till May." Chunk closed his eyes and started absorbing the rays. I pulled a piece of grass out of the turf and chewed on it. It was weird, thinking about next May. High school would be ending for good, and a new life would begin. The big question was, would Rena Steuben be part of that life? And what about Howie?

From the corner of the field the ball floated up in the air, growing larger. A group of players pushed and shoved each other in front of me, but they were only a blur of yellow scrimmage jerseys and white T-shirts in my peripheral vision. All eyes were on the ball as it shot toward us.

Two bodies suddenly flew above the others— Chunk trying to head the ball out of the goal mouth and Billy Lee trying to head it in. Once the ball hit, there would be no time to react, so I jumped to my right hoping the ball would ricochet that way. There was a grunting crash as Billy and Chunk collided, and the ball flew just inches beyond my fingertips.

"Yellow goal!" yelled Coach Lavelle, who was acting as ref for the scrimmage.

In front of the goal Chunk helped Billy to his feet. "Pure luck," he kidded. Billy Lee just smiled. Maybe it had been lucky, but Billy had been in the right place at the right time to get lucky. I turned back to get the ball out of the net and found Rena standing behind the goal with her friend Sara Parker.

"You could have dived," she said.

"Rena!" Surprise. I couldn't remember the last time she'd come to a practice.

"We wanted to see how the team looked," Sara said. She was Rena's best friend and was considered, by those who cared about such things, the most popular girl in our class. I couldn't stand her.

"What do you think?" I asked.

"I think you could have gotten it if you'd dived," Rena said.

"Hey, Gilbert," someone yelled, "quit talking to your girl friends and get the ball." I picked up the ball, threw it into the midfield, and got back into position.

Since the yellows had just scored, it was the T-shirts' turn to take the ball, and I noticed a new enthusiasm among my scrimmage mates. It's funny how play improves when girls come to watch, even if it's only a practice or a scrimmage. It makes you wonder if they've ever done any experiments comparing an athlete's performance when no one is watching to his performance in front of girls. Or maybe that's the whole idea behind cheerleaders.

Anyway, as soon as Rena and Sara left, the enthusiasm among the players immediately disappeared. Coach Lavelle stood in the middle of the field, scratching his head while players loafed after balls they'd previously sprinted for. "Come on, you guys," he shouted. "Just because there's no one to show off for doesn't mean practice is over." But no one ran any faster.

Later, back in the locker room, Chunk and I were pulling off our sweaty soccer duds. "What do you think of Sara Parker?" he asked.

What did I think of Sara? That she was a Gold Coast princess, that she had to be the best at everything she did, and nothing but the best was good enough for her. Despite my personal opinion, I knew that most guys thought Sara was prettier than Rena. Sara was more popular too. Where Rena could sometimes be ill-tempered and moody, Sara always pretended to be cheerful and friendly even when you knew she wanted to kill. Everything she did had to be the right thing to do. She actually dressed better than the women teachers at Cooper's Neck High and drove a new orange Corvette, which no teacher could afford. Even when she smoked dope she used a fancy gold roach clip that I bet came from Cartier or someplace like that.

Someone in the next aisle over was banging his soccer shoe against his locker, probably trying to get the mud out from between the cleats. "Hey!" Chunk yelled. "Cut it out."

"Eat me," came the retort. It was Johnny Jarret,

38

starting fullback and general grossout. The banging continued.

"I'll come over there and shove that shoe down your throat," Chunk growled.

Jarret's response was a low, gurgling grumble, and Chunk and I had just enough time to jump out of the way before a thick glob of phlegm arched over the lockers and splatted on the bench where we'd been sitting. Chunk went around the corner while I picked up a dirty T-shirt from the floor and wiped the phlegm away.

Sounds of commotion flew over the lockers. "Oh, no, Chunk, I was only kidding. Ow . . . OW . . . OW!"

Chunk returned to his seat next to me on the bench. "Jerk," he muttered. He started unwrapping his right ankle. "So what do you think?"

"About Sara?"

"Yeah."

"You're crazy."

Chunk nodded. "I swear I didn't start it. But about a week ago I noticed she was giving me the eye. I mean the heavy eye."

"It's your tan, Chunk."

"What?"

"You're tanner than she is," I said. "You know she can't stand anyone being tanner than her."

Chunk shrugged. "You ever see her come to a practice before?"

"Uh, no." He had a point there.

Chunk pulled off his jock and scratched himself, probably the way he thought a cowboy would scratch himself. "Well, I think there's something in the wind, partner."

I smiled. Knowing Chunk, I wasn't about to bet against it.

CHAPTER
SIX

The following week I went back to the hospital to see Howie again. It was the day before the Seaport match, and Coach Lavelle took us through a light practice and let us go early—no sense in tiring everyone out before a game.

Even as I got into my mother's car and headed for the hospital, I wasn't exactly sure why I was going. No one had asked me to go this time, but I knew part of the reason had to do with my general curiosity about medicine. Then there was Howie. I still felt bad about his being all alone. I guess I knew that if I didn't go, no one else would. Maybe some of my mother's humanitarianism was rubbing off on me.

Anyway, Howie should have been finishing up the treatment and getting ready to go home, and I thought it would be a nice surprise if I dropped by. I didn't plan to stay long, only to stop in and say hello.

At the Solomon Cohen Pavilion the door to Howie's room was closed, and I knocked and pushed it open, thinking only about surprising him. But inside, something was wrong. I heard someone sniff and turned to find Mrs. Jamison clutching a ragged piece of tissue and dabbing her eyes.

The first thing I thought was, *Howie died!* But I turned to the bed and saw him lying there watching me. There was something different about his face, but I didn't register it because my eyes focused on a strange green mat of tubes lying on his chest.

"Maybe I ought to go, huh?" I said.

Howie didn't say anything. I realized his face was swollen, as if he'd been stung by a bee and had an allergic reaction.

"No, please stay," Mrs. Jamison said. She stopped crying. I looked at her, wondering what had happened. "Howie has to stay in the hospital," she said "He has an infection."

I looked at Howie again, but he looked away and didn't say anything. So much for my surprise visit, I thought.

"He was supposed to go home tomorrow," his mother said. "But he caught something right here in the hospital. The doctors say he's more susceptible to infections, but why do they keep him here, where there are all kinds of sick people?"

"Uh . . ." I felt like I was supposed to answer her, but I didn't know what to say.

"I can't go home, Mom," Howie said weakly. "They've got to keep an eye on me, and I need this thing." He nodded toward the green mat. I noticed that the mat was attached to a small machine that pumped liquid through the tubes.

"What is that, Howie?" I asked.

"It's a hypothermia blanket," he said. "It has cold water and alcohol circulating through the tubes to keep my temperature down."

"He had a temperature of one hundred and five this afternoon," Mrs. Jamison said.

"Big deal," Howie grumbled.

For a couple of moments no one said anything. Howie looked pale; he was still hooked up to the IV. Mrs. Jamison's eye makeup was a little smeared. I sort of regretted being there in the middle of it all, but now that I was in the room I figured I'd better stay. A guy in a white outfit, an orderly, came in and looked at a tray of food that was on the table next to Howie's bed.

"Should I leave it?" he asked. Nothing on the tray had been touched.

Howie shook his head, and the orderly took the tray and left.

"David," Mrs. Jamison said, "have you ever heard of Laetrile?"

"It sounds familiar."

"It's a drug that's being used in Mexico to fight

cancer. You go on a special high-protein diet. They're starting to use it in the United States now. My sister lives in Texas, and she told me about it last night. She said it's legal in several states. I think she said Florida."

"Geez, Mom," Howie moaned. "That's the stuff made from apricot seeds. It's worthless."

"Mary Ellen says the recovery rate is just as high as when people go through . . . through this." She fumbled for words.

"Oh, man," Howie moaned again. "I gotta get into the john." He slid the green mat off and quickly slipped out of bed and into the bathroom. Even with the door closed I could hear him retching.

Mrs. Jamison and I looked at each other. "David, please come here," she said softly. I sat down next to her, and she took one of my hands and pressed it between hers. Her eyes were filling with water again. "I don't think I can stand it," she blurted out. "I know I have to be strong for Howie, but he puts me through such difficult tests. Sometimes he searches my face." She sniffed. "I feel him looking into me for the answers to all these questions we have. I try to be strong, but I have feelings too. I just don't think I'll be able to stand it if he doesn't come home soon."

The next thing I knew, Mrs. Jamison put her face against my shoulder and started to cry. It was the first time in my life an adult had done that. And I hardly even knew her. I swallowed nervously and patted her on the back. "He'll get better, Mrs. Jamison. I know he will."

"You really think so?" she asked, wiping her eyes.

"Sure," I said. "He's a tough kid." But inside I was wondering why she should believe me.

The door of the bathroom began to open, and I quickly let go of Mrs. Jamison and got up. I didn't want Howie to see me holding his mother. I didn't know why exactly, it just seemed weird. Howie walked slowly from the bathroom. The front of his hospital gown was all wet. I watched as he climbed uncertainly into the bed and pulled the hypothermia blanket over him again. He looked at us for a moment, and I saw a bit of a spark in his eyes. "I don't mind the fit," he said, shifting the green mat until it was comfortable. "But I can't stand the color."

Even his mother smiled a little.

I stayed until visiting hours ended and then told Howie I'd come back to the hospital soon. For the first time that evening he seemed genuinely glad for a few moments. Then I waited outside the room while Mrs. Jamison spoke to her son alone.

"You don't know how much he appreciates your coming," Mrs. Jamison said later as we walked down the hall from Howie's room. "It's so difficult for us, being new up here and all."

"How's Mr. Jamison?" I asked. I was wondering why I hadn't seen him at the hospital.

"He's coping as best he can. He sees Howie in the morning for an hour, but he's got an awful lot of work in the office, and he's new there. It's not a good idea for him to take off too much time." She paused for a moment. "But it's very hard for him, what with Howie being our only child."

I wanted to put my arm around her and give her a supportive hug, but I didn't because I wasn't sure how she would take it. Outside it had started raining, and I waited while Mrs. Jamison took a little plastic rain hood out of her bag and pulled it over her head. We walked out to the parking lot.

"I just want Howie home again," she said, stepping around a puddle in the lot. She sounded really low.

"I bet he'll be home sooner than you think," I said.

Mrs. Jamison nodded. "I hope so, David."

I watched her get into her station wagon and then I walked across the lot to my mother's car. But before I got in, I looked back at the tall brick and concrete hospital complex. Most of the buildings were new and modern-looking, and I recalled the newspaper stories about all the fantastic things they were supposed to be doing in there. They even had their own helicopter landing pad for emergency cases. Great, I thought, but can you make Howie Jamison well again?

At home my mother had kept dinner warm for me. For the last twelve years my mother had been teaching art to first and second graders at the Cooper's Neck grade school. Twelve years of stick figures, clay ashtrays, and kids drinking paint all day. Then she'd come home and cook dinner every night. It was a lot different from the way most Gold Coast mothers lived. Rena's mother, for instance, spent so much time in department stores that she sent Christmas cards to the salesgirls every year. And Chunk's mother played tennis two or three hours a day, summer and winter. My mother's exercise consisted of chasing kids around the classroom, shopping, and cooking.

"How is Howie?" she asked.

"He's got some kind of infection and they can't let him go home," I said, sitting down at the dinner table. "His mom is really upset."

"I can imagine," my mother said. She sat down at the table with me. I could tell there was something bothering her. "David," she said, "I think what you're doing, visiting Howie, is a very fine thing. But I want you to be careful. Don't eat anything in the room, and try not to touch anything Howie's touched. I don't want to scare you, but science knows very little about cancer."

"You mean I *could* get it?" I asked.

"Nobody really knows," she said. "The chances appear very slim, but there is such a thing as a cancer cluster, where a lot of children in one area are stricken."

"But isn't that because the water or air in that area is polluted?" I asked.

"It could be, David," she said. "I don't want you to stop seeing Howie. I just don't want you to take any unnecessary risks."

"I won't, Mom," I said. I had a feeling neither she nor I knew what constituted an "unnecessary risk," but it made me feel a little strange anyway.

My mother watched while I gobbled down several pieces of barbecued chicken and a lot of rice. I was pretty sure I knew what she was thinking: She was glad I was healthy and able to eat my food too fast, rather than sick. It took something like Howie getting leukemia to make you realize you were lucky just to be healthy.

"David," she said a few moments later. "Last week you said something about not wanting to go to a school that could give you a soccer scholarship. Why?"

I looked at my mother and tapped a half-eaten drumstick against my plate. Up till now only

Rena knew about my pre-med plans. I guess I hadn't told a lot of people because I wanted to be certain first. But visiting Howie made me more certain. Each time I saw him I wished there was something more I could do than just sit there and watch. "I want to go to a college with a good pre-med program that'll help me get into medical school," I said.

My mother blinked. "When did you decide this?" she asked.

"Last year."

She shook her head. I think that if she'd known how wide her smile was, she would have worked on making it smaller. She'd never been crazy about my plans to be a pro soccer player. As far as she was concerned, I had only three choices in life: law, medicine, and failure. Basically, she would have preferred it if I was more like my sister, Cheryl, who was married to a workaholic sales manager for a big printing company and lived in a house about twice the size of ours in New Canaan, Connecticut. So telling my mother I wanted to be a doctor sort of made her life complete, especially by Gold Coast standards.

"I don't see what you're so happy about," I said. "If I do it, it's gonna cost you a lot of money you weren't planning to spend."

My mother's smile shrank into an amused smirk. "Are you worried we can't afford it?"

"I think Dad was kind of expecting me to get a scholarship."

My mother reached over and affectionately squeezed my cheek between her thumb and forefinger. "I think he'll understand," she said.

CHAPTER
SEVEN

The next day we smeared Seaport High 5–0, which in soccer is a slaughter. There was a rumor going around that an assistant coach from Southern Illinois University, with a pocket full of soccer scholarships, was there watching the game. If he was, he must have been impressed. But when I looked toward the sidelines, I wasn't looking for him, I was looking for Rena. She finally showed up late in the second half and spent the rest of the game down at the other end of the field, shooting pictures of Billy Lee, who scored four goals and played out of his mind.

Ever since I'd started going with Rena I hardly ever got my picture in the school newspaper. I suspected that was because she was sensitive to accusations of favoritism. Sometimes I didn't mind. Like, that day, Billy deserved to be photographed. But there were other times when I knew I deserved a photo and it always hurt a little when I didn't get it.

After the game Rena was waiting to give me a ride home, so I cleared it with Lavelle. The team rule was, we had to take the school bus to the game to make sure everyone was there for warm-ups, but we were allowed to go home by any means we wanted. I threw my sports bag in the back of Rena's VW Rabbit and got in the front seat to drive. Rena sat beside me.

"Was Billy this good last year?" Rena asked as we drove home on the Expressway.

"Not really."

"What did he do over the summer?"

"I think he was a counselor at Mike Stone's soccer camp," I said. Billy was a true soccer fanatic. His goal in life was to be America's first Oriental pro soccer player.

"Does it bother you?"

"What?"

"That he's gotten so much better," Rena said.

"No."

Rena was quiet for a moment. "Last year it would have."

"I guess I've changed," I said, steering the car off the Expressway and onto an exit ramp.

Rena didn't reply and I started thinking about Howie. I'd meant to tell him about smoking grass during my visit the day before, but the opportunity hadn't come up. I'd have to tell him the next time

I saw him. Funny, but I was certain I'd be seeing him again soon. Maybe I'd even call him that night to tell him the outcome of the game. I was sure he'd be interested.

We came to a red light, and I looked at Rena. "I went back to the hospital yesterday to see that guy I told you about—Howie. It's so incredible what he's going through, Rena. I mean, you're wondering whether I care that Billy Lee is a better soccer player than me, and I'm sitting here wondering if Howie is ever going to be well again. Can you imagine going through that? Right now he's lying there, not even knowing if he's going to be alive next year."

Rena stared back at me. I guess she didn't know what to say. The light turned green, but I leaned over and kissed her on the cheek before moving. "Hey, I'm glad you made it today."

Rena nodded, unsmiling.

To get from the Expressway to my house you had to pass a large pond with a small park next to it. It was almost dusk now, the sun was low and bright yellow-orange over the trees on the far side of the pond. I pulled the car into the park.

"You in a rush?" I asked, wanting to spend a little more time with her.

Rena shook her head and reached for one of her cameras as we got out of the car. We had often come to this park during the summer before, and Rena would experiment with the sunlight reflected off the glassy pond water while I did homework for my summer courses. We walked down to the water and I lay on my back, looking up at the clouds turning bright pink in the sunset. Rena sat near me, the camera at her eye. I watched her, thinking she was the prettiest girl I had ever gone out with. The features of her face were sharp but fine, and her skin was always pale, making her seem delicate. But that was only a disguise for the strong-willed, determined, and independent person underneath.

I was beginning to understand why Rena sometimes acted like she didn't care if I broke a date with her and why she so easily forgot about the team's first match of the year. It was her way of keeping some distance between us. That might seem pretty weird, considering that I was her boyfriend, but I was starting to see that Rena didn't want to be as involved with me as I was with her. There was a part of her she didn't want me to touch. It was almost as if she was an actress, just acting the girl friend, while I was left wondering when the play would close.

"Rena?"

"Hmm?" Her eye remained at the camera's eyepiece.

"Sometimes I wish you'd tell me what you're thinking," I said.

"I'm just looking at the pond," she said.

"You know, before, when I said that Howie

doesn't know if he's going to be alive a year from now, it made me realize I don't even know what's going to happen to *us* a year from now."

Rena put down her camera and looked at me. "What do you mean?" she asked.

"I mean, you haven't even told me where you're applying to college."

"Vassar, Yale, Brown, maybe more."

I waited, hoping she would ask me where I was going to apply. I'd thought of suggesting that we go to schools near each other (our grades were too far apart to go to the same school). If we were nearby, at least we could see each other once in a while. It pained me a little that Rena hadn't even thought of that. I sat up and said, "We could wind up at colleges three thousand miles apart."

Rena nodded. She had this funny look on her face. Maybe she thought I was going to ask her to marry me or something.

"Do you want that to happen?" I asked.

"I haven't thought it out clearly yet."

"Great," I said. "What am I supposed to do now, check in each day to see if you've started thinking clearly yet?"

Her eyes moved slowly away from me. "David, I wish you wouldn't be so serious all the time."

I got up and walked past her, down to the edge of the pond. It was frustrating. "You never give me a straight answer, Rena. You just treat me like I'm a dumb jock who shouldn't know any better."

I stood there, feeling angry and looking at the muddy pond water until I felt her arms go around me and her breasts push against my back as she hugged me from behind. She kissed me on the neck and I felt goose bumps run down my arms. It made it hard to keep my mind on the subject.

CHAPTER EIGHT

A few days later Rena told me we were invited to a dinner party Sara was giving and that the "men" would be required to wear ties and jackets. Typical Sara. Rena thought I'd be surprised to learn who Sara's date for the evening was.

"Didn't you once tell me Sara thinks athletes are smelly and crude?" I said.

"That was before she found out that some of them make a million dollars a year," Rena replied.

Sara's party was supposed to start at seven o'clock, so Rena and I arrived around eight. Judging from Sara's welcome, our timing was appropriate. Sara's house was famous around the Gold Coast. It was very modern, all stone and glass on the outside, very expensive (my father guessed about half a million bucks), and very comfortable inside. Sara's mother's sole purpose in life seemed to be keeping it perfectly clean and getting stories about it into magazines like *Town & Country, House Beautiful,* and *Architectural Digest.* Copies of all the magazines that had done stories about the house were displayed prominently on coffee tables, like little trophies.

As much as I disliked what Sara's house represented, I had to admit that the house itself really was beautiful. We joined the other guests sitting on sofas and chairs around a big stone hearth in which a fire crackled. If you sat sideways to the hearth, you could look out the big windows along the back of the house and see past the backyard to the thin strip of sandy beach and water beyond. It reminded me of a castle by the sea. And Sara was definitely its princess.

It was a small dinner party, only four couples. Besides Chunk and Sara and Rena and me, there were Robert Tuckel, his girl friend Sally, Karl Stearn and his date, Colette, who we called Cole for short. I didn't know Sally or Cole very well but Karl, who was the editor of the school newspaper, was a pretty nice guy. Tuckel, however, was a real jerk. He was into the artsy Andy Warhol scene and he was always making idiotic remarks about art and socialism and New Wave this and New Wave that. He even had New Wave hair with a streak of emerald green dyed into it. And he wore a black leather jacket and two ties, one brown lizard skin and the other green rubber. He professed to be some kind of genius artist, but he was mostly in dumb classes, and the only talent I could see was for talking.

Sara served hors d'oeuvres, and Chunk volunteered to make the drinks. He was wearing a blazer, with a checked western shirt underneath, blue jeans, and cowboy boots. On top of it all was his favorite cowboy hat. (Sara's interest in millionaires aside, I couldn't help thinking that part of her interest in Chunk was to compete with Rena. After all, going with the team captain was one better than dating the goalie.) Beer was conspicuously absent, so we had scotch and sodas while the girls drank white wine. Tuckel insisted on vodka straight, on the rocks, but I noticed he took only one sip and didn't touch his glass again.

As usual, Sara treated us as if we were a bunch of kids and she was the supervising parent. She made Chunk take off his cowboy hat and seemed amused by Tuckel's outfit. She gave you the feeling that this dinner party was simply practice for the day when she would give a *real* dinner party for *real* people. I resented the way she treated us, but I couldn't deny that even in practice she was pretty good. The dinner table was set with small vases of flowers and we ate by candlelight. I had a feeling that what Sara was calling grouse were really those little Cornish hens my mother bought in the supermarket, but they were delicious. After dinner Sara served coffee and brandy.

The conversation, unfortunately, was much less tasty than dinner. Tuckel, as usual, did most of the talking. Tonight's subject was suicide, which, I knew from previous parties, was one of his favorite topics. According to Tuckel, suicide was perfectly acceptable to an artist who viewed his life like a work of art and knew when it was finished.

Chunk scowled at me. I guess he wasn't used to that kind of conversation. I was thinking about Howie. At least Tuckel's artist had a choice about living or dying.

I knew Rena would agree with Tuckel because committing suicide was an act of free will, and Rena was into free will. I'd been tempted at times to ask her if she knew of anyone who wasn't into free will, but I didn't want to fight. Sometime during the continuing conversation Chunk yawned, and Sara blushed. Cole seemed to go to the bathroom every five minutes, and Karl looked bored.

Then Sally, Tuckel's girl friend, said, "Does anyone know about that boy who transferred from Florida? My mother says he's dying of cancer."

"How ghastly," Sara said. Don't ask me why Sara used words like that.

"David knows him," Rena said.

Suddenly everyone was staring at me. "Well, I've only met him a couple of times," I said. I really didn't think it was anyone's business, but

60

it was obvious that they all wanted to hear about it. "He's getting treated for leukemia. I don't think you should say he's dying."

They were quiet for a moment. Then Tuckel said, "Cancer kills more people in this country than any other disease. It's the Big C, man."

"Actually, heart disease kills more people, Bobby," Karl Stearn said.

"My mother says he has a form of leukemia that hardly anyone recovers from," Sally said.

That really ticked me off. "Come off it, Sally, how does your mother know what form of leukemia Howie has?"

"It's got some initials," she said. "Like AML or something."

I was about to tell her that she was full of it when I remembered that Mrs. Jamison had said something about AML the first day I'd seen Howie in the hospital. I tried to remember what she'd said . . . "Not the worst, but not the best either." How did Sally's mother know? I wondered.

"What kind of treatment is he getting?" Karl asked.

"Some kind of chemotherapy," I said.

"Oh yeah." Chunk suddenly spoke up. He'd been practically silent all evening and I guess he was eager to contribute. "My aunt had that before she died. My mother says all it did was prolong the agony."

Sara rolled her eyes dramatically. "Must we have this depressing conversation?" she asked.

No one said anything for a few moments. I wasn't sure why, but I was beginning to feel pissed off at everyone at the party. It must have been the way they were talking about Howie. Like he was just another piece of gossip you chewed over for a while and then spit out when it was no longer tasty. It didn't seem to matter to them that he was a real human being.

Then Tuckel said, "He should have the right to die without the agony. If I had cancer, I think I'd just take a super overdose of heroin and get it over with quick."

"I saw a TV show about a woman who did that," Sally said. "She had breast cancer and decided she didn't want to go through the treatment and have her breast removed, so she wrote letters to all her friends, saying she was going to kill herself. She even had a party the night before she did it. It was weird."

"But there are a lot of forms of cancer that aren't fatal," I said. "He's supposed to come home any day now."

"God, do you think they'll let him come to school?" Sally asked.

"If he gets the same treatment my aunt had, he won't even be able to get out of bed," Chunk said.

"If I couldn't get any heroin," Tuckel was saying, "I'd just shoot a big air bubble into my vein.

That's how the CIA kills people without getting caught."

"Just a minute, please," I said.

But no one heard me—Tuckel was still babbling about the CIA and air bubbles.

"Wait a minute." This time I said it a little louder. At the same time my leg accidentally hit the table. Sara gasped as all the glasses and silverware rattled. One little vase of flowers fell over and the water inside spilled onto the tablecloth. I quickly righted it. "Sorry about that," I said to Sara, who looked for a brief moment like she wanted to kill me. But at least I had everyone's attention. "I just wanted to say that Howie really is sick. I mean, while we're sitting here talking about him, he's over in West Hill really going through it. I think if you could see him, you wouldn't talk about committing suicide, because it's the last thing in the world Howie's thinking of, I promise you."

Under the table Rena poked my leg, but I wasn't finished. "You ought to remember that he's all alone in this hospital in this strange place where he doesn't know anyone. I know he only came to school for one week, but maybe some of you ought to go see him. I'm serious. You'd get as much out of seeing Howie as he would from seeing you." Across the table Sally shook her head. "Sally," I said. "You don't have to worry. Leukemia's not contagious. And if he does come back to school, I hope you won't treat him like an outcast or anything. He's just like any of us, except he's sick and trying to get better. I mean, how would you feel if you got cancer and everybody treated you like you were a lost cause?"

I looked around the table, but everyone seemed to look away just before our eyes met, until I got to Sally. "Well, I don't see what you're making such a big deal about," she said. "I thought you said you've only seen him a couple of times."

"Yeah, I, uh . . ." I didn't know what to say. Didn't Sally understand? It didn't matter how many times I'd seen Howie or how well anyone knew or didn't know him. The point was, Howie was there in the hospital, and he was alone.

Sara managed to steer the conversation away from Howie by asking Chunk how he thought the soccer team would do this year. Even Tuckel couldn't come up with a way to connect soccer with suicide. When the party ended about an hour later, Sara seemed infinitely relieved.

Outside, it was dark and chilly. Rena and I walked to my mother's car, but she stopped a few feet away from it.

"I don't understand you, David," she said. "Last week this Howie person didn't exist. Now he's all you can talk about."

"I know, Rena. I can't explain it. There's just something about him being all alone and having to go through this. It's not fair. I really feel like he needs friends."

"But do you think it's fair to insist that we all go see him?" she asked.

"I didn't mean to make an issue out of it, Rena. I just thought it would be nice for Howie."

"But we don't even know him, David." Rena held a handful of her long hair and twisted the ends in her fingers. "I don't understand what's happened to you all of a sudden," she said. "Last year you wanted to become a professional soccer player. It seemed so important to you. It was a challenge, and something different from everyone else around here who just wants to grow up and be a millionaire."

"Or marry one," I added for her.

Rena made a face. "Then you went to summer school and suddenly decided to become a doctor. That's so typical. Sixty percent of our class will be doctors and lawyers. It's almost an annual statistic. I thought you'd be different. But now you just want to be like everyone else. You just want to conform."

"You would prefer I dyed my hair green and wore rubber ties like Tuckel?"

Rena sighed. "Bobby is different. He needs to be different."

"So he's just conforming to whatever is different," I said.

Rena didn't answer. She was probably wondering how we ever got on the subject of Tuckel. So was I. For a few moments we just looked at each other in the dark. Rena looked cold. "Would you take me home?" she asked.

Rena lived up in Cooper's Point in a big red-brick house hidden from the road by a tall hedge and surrounded by a lawn so perfectly manicured that you were afraid an alarm might go off if you stepped on it. I parked the car in the gravel drive-way and left the engine running. There were only a couple of lights on in the house, the ones Mrs. Steuben usually left on when she went to the city for the night.

In the car Rena sat next to me, smoking. Neither of us spoke until she finished the cigarette and crushed it out in the ashtray.

"Do you want me to come in?" I asked. It was the first time in a long time that I'd felt I had to ask.

Rena looked down at her lap. "I don't know, David."

"Well," I said, putting the car in reverse, "then I guess I better not."

CHAPTER
NINE

Howie came home from the hospital the next weekend and asked me over for dinner Saturday night. Rena was in the city for the day and Penn State had flown Chunk down to meet their soccer coach, so I was glad for the invitation. As I walked up the Jamisons' driveway I saw Howie standing at the front door, wearing a bathrobe and pajamas, looking thin and frail, but smiling as he watched me. "Hey, dude." We shook hands.

Tempting aromas wafted through the doorway. "Smells good," I said as Howie ushered me in.

"My mom went to get my dad at the train station," Howie said. "He had to work in the city today. Hope you're ready for some real southern cooking."

"Fried chicken?"

Howie grinned. "You were expecting maybe

Hungarian goulash?" He started walking slowly toward the living room. It was the first time I'd been in the Jamisons' house and even though they'd been living in Cooper's Neck Estates for nearly two months, it still looked bare and unlived in. Paintings that were meant to be hung on the walls still lay on the floor, and a couple of rugs were rolled up in a corner. New brass drapery rods had been put up over the windows, but no drapes hung from them. It seemed a little odd to me.

Howie eased down into a couch and I sat near him in a chair. The sleeve of his robe slipped to his elbow and I almost jumped out of my seat when I saw his forearm—all black and blue and yellow and red from transfusions, injections, and blood tests.

"I'm supposed to be in remission now," Howie said. "I gotta go in for tests once a week and later this month I'll go in for five days of maintenance chemotherapy, but otherwise I'm just supposed to get my strength back. The doctor said I can go back to school when I feel up to it."

"That's great, Howie." I'd done a little research on my own and I knew that remissions, when the disease was not active in the body, did not always last. If Howie's remission ended, he'd have to go back to the hospital for the whole treatment again. Except each time you came out of remission it took more drugs and agony to get you back in.

While Howie and I talked I noticed a book lying on the coffee table near the couch. Its title was *Fight Against Death*, and the blurb said it was about a man who gets cancer and fights it even after his doctors have given up. Howie saw me looking at it.

"My mom got it out of the library," he said. "She's got a couple more of them upstairs. You know, exposés on the real truth about cancer and how doctors and scientists are deluding the public. Lot of garbage I wish she wouldn't read."

"Gives her bad ideas?"

"Yeah," Howie said. "And I don't feel like I'm fighting death. I feel like I'm sick and fighting to get better. Besides, I trust doctors. I know they make mistakes sometimes, but I think they know more than these people who want you to take apricot seeds and carrot juice. The thing is, whenever there's a problem, like when I get an infection or have a seizure, my mother thinks it's the doctor's fault. That he could have done something to prevent it. I'll tell you, what scares me isn't so much the doctor as the way she's getting lately, like it's a big plot against us. Every time something goes wrong, she looks for some sinister motive."

We heard the garage door bang open. "That's them," Howie said. I was glad his parents were home, because the smell of that food was making me really hungry. Mr. Jamison came in, wearing a business suit and carrying a briefcase. He was taller than Howie and had darker hair and thick eyebrows. There were deep creases in the skin around his mouth and on his forehead.

"Hello, David." He shook my hand. "How's the soccer team doing?" Howie must have told him about that.

"Undefeated," I said.

Mr. Jamison turned toward Howie, who'd remained seated. "And how's the patient?"

"Undefeated," Howie replied.

Mrs. Jamison had gone into the kitchen to check on dinner and now she called everyone in. We crowded into the kitchen and sat down around a white Formica table with molded plastic chairs that reminded me of a set my parents had when I was a kid. There were two big pieces of chicken and big blobs of mashed potatoes on each plate. The chicken was really delicious and crisp and I told Mrs. Jamison so. Howie and his father quickly concurred, and for a few minutes Mrs. Jamison was beaming and happy.

But Howie could barely eat his food, and his mother began to look worried. Soon Mr. Jamison and I had finished the food on our plates and it was pretty obvious that Howie wasn't going to come close to finishing his.

"Howie, eat some more," Mrs. Jamison said in a coaxing way, as if he were a little boy.

"I'm not feeling very hungry today," Howie said.

"Just a little more, Howie," his mother said anxiously.

We watched Howie force another forkful of potatoes into his mouth and chew them slowly, as if he couldn't bring himself to swallow. "I think I got so used to that lousy hospital food that it's gonna take some time to adjust to good cooking," he said. His mother was not amused, but she got up and served Mr. Jamison and me cups of tapioca pudding. I ate the pudding slowly, pretending that I was full and having a hard time stuffing it down.

Meanwhile, Mrs. Jamison sat quietly, watching her son. You could see that she was getting upset. Howie managed to take another bite or two of his chicken, but that was the limit. He couldn't force himself to eat any more. Howie's mother was just about to say something when Mr. Jamison interrupted her. "The doctor said it might take Howie some time to get his appetite back because of the treatments, Beth. I'm sure he'll eat more tomorrow."

Mr. Jamison's mention of Howie's treatment reminded me of something. "You know, if you smoke marijuana while you're having chemotherapy, it helps."

Howie looked at me, his mouth a little agape.

71

"You're not really serious, David," Mrs. Jamison said.

"Yes I am, really," I said.

Mrs. Jamison looked at her husband. Mr. Jamison looked at me. "How, David?"

"Well, I don't know exactly. But it's supposed to ease some of the side effects."

Mrs. Jamison had a strange look on her face, as if she wasn't sure whether to laugh or not. Mr. Jamison was scowling. I realized they didn't believe me at all. For a while we just sat around the table, no one talking. Howie kept looking from his parents to me. The strain had to be on all our faces. We'd tried to have a normal dinner together, but it wasn't possible. Maybe it was wrong to even try. And now I felt like an idiot for mentioning the marijuana. Mrs. Jamison was still looking at me like I was nuts.

Howie suddenly pushed his chair back and stood up. "I want to go out for a walk with David," he announced to his startled parents.

"Now, Howie?" his father said. "It's dark out."

"I've been out in the dark before," Howie said.

"Howie, please don't go out now," his mother practically begged.

But Howie insisted. "Don't you know that the only time I've been outside for the last month was to walk back and forth from the car to the hospital? I don't care if it's dark or not. I'm not going that far. Even the doctor said it was okay for me to get out."

You could see that Mr. Jamison was caught between his concern for his son and his desire to make him happy by granting his smallest wish. "But why in the dark, Howie?" he asked.

"Because I *feel* like it," Howie said emphatically. "Don't worry, I'm not gonna get mugged."

"We just don't want you to get—uh—catch another infection," his mother said.

"Okay, I'll get bundled up good," Howie said. "I'm only going for a short walk. Come on, Dad, let me go."

Mr. Jamison looked at me. "You'll be careful?"

I nodded, but I wondered what Mr. Jamison thought I could protect Howie from here in Cooper's Neck Estates. The raccoons? Howie went up to his room and put on pants, a sweater, and his winter parka. I didn't tell him he was over-dressing, but I had to stifle a smile when Mrs. Jamison brought out a wool cap from the closet. I guess it's true about southerners having a hard time getting used to the cold.

"Please don't stay out too long," Mrs. Jamison said. She looked as if she might fall apart at any moment, and if I had been Howie, that look alone might have been enough to stop my walk. But maybe Howie knew something I was still trying to figure out, that no matter how close to the brink she looked, she'd never go over. She only wanted you to think she would.

We'd hardly gotten out the door, before Howie's parents started fighting. For a second I thought something was wrong, but Howie just mumbled, "I knew it," and kept walking. As I followed him down the driveway it was impossible to ignore what his mother was yelling, because one of the kitchen windows was open. First it was about the marijuana, then about the neighbors not being friendly and the hospital only wanting their money. We could also hear Mr. Jamison trying to calm her down, telling her to take something the doctor had given her. It must have been embarrassing for Howie, and we walked a little faster. The last thing I heard Mrs. Jamison say was, *"I don't know why we ever left Florida!"*

It was a clear evening and there was a faint cool breeze carrying the smell of saltwater inland. In the sky there was just a hint of light left from the sunset, but down under the scattered trees it was dark. We left the new asphalt driveway and stepped onto the new asphalt street. The way Howie was dressed you would have thought he was heading for the North Pole.

He turned left, staying on the road shoulder, and I followed.

I guess Howie wanted to get out of earshot of his house before he stopped and said, "I can't believe you told my parents I should smoke pot."

"But it's true, Howie."

He nodded. "I know. A doctor at the hospital told me. But my parents . . ." He shook his head slowly. "You can't tell them stuff like that. My mother probably thinks you'll want to sell me some heroin next."

"I'm sorry, Howie. It didn't even occur to me. I mean, around here more parents smoke dope than kids."

"Yeah, well, it ain't like the South, boy."

For a while neither of us said a thing. We just walked, keeping to the side of the street. Then Howie stopped and looked up. "I haven't seen the moon in months."

"How's it look?" I asked.

"Uh, like the moon." But he kept staring at it as if he was surprised to see it there. Then he looked back down the street toward his parents' house. "I had to get out tonight," he said. "They never used to fight like that. It's like . . . this is gonna sound weird, David. It's like I feel it's my fault that they're so unhappy, you know? I feel guilty for getting sick, because it makes them so miserable. Sometimes I think if I went away to someplace like the moon for a while, they'd feel better. How come I'm sick but I feel like I'm the one who's making them so unhappy?"

I didn't know how to answer him. What Howie was saying made sense, but it sounded crazy too. Nothing in my life had ever hinted that someday

I might know someone with a disease like leukemia. The only times I'd even heard of leukemia were in books and on some dumb soap opera I'd watched on TV one day when I'd stayed home from school. It hadn't ever occurred to me that *real* people could catch it. But here was Howie Jamison, still too healthy for me to believe he could really be *that* sick, but at the same time too sick for me to ignore the truth. I felt helpless, just like that day Mrs. Jamison had cried on my shoulder in the hospital.

"They understand it's not your fault," I said.

"They understand it," Howie said, "but I'm not sure . . . I'm not sure *I* understand it. Sometimes I feel like I got sick because I'm being punished for being bad. Jacked off too many times or something like that. Like I've sinned."

That surprised me. "You really think you're being punished?"

"No . . . yes and no." Howie started to walk again. "I don't really believe in God or anything, but I've got some of that good old southern Christian fear of the Lord ingrained in me. I guess it comes from my mother's parents. They were real Sunday churchgoers. My mother used to be one too, but me and my dad never went, so she sort of stopped. But since I got sick she's been talking about it again. And it gets kind of infectious, like the next thing I know, I start looking for a reason why I'm sick. Asking myself why me? Why not someone else. Why not you?" Howie faltered for a second and then slapped me on the back. "Hey, I wasn't serious. Never in a million years would I want this to happen to anyone else, especially you."

I tried to smile at him, but his words scared me. If Howie could get cancer, there was no reason why I couldn't get it too. And why had it been Howie and not me?

"All I meant," Howie continued, "was that when I start asking why me, the only logical answer I get is, because I deserve it. Sometimes when my imagination really gets cranked up, I start reviewing my life, adding up all the bad things I've done to see if enough of them could mean I deserve this."

We were walking toward the back of Cooper's Neck Estates, up where the houses were still unfinished and there were no streetlights. It was really dark up there.

"What's crazy is, I have no way of knowing," Howie was saying. "I mean, does hocking a couple of albums, lying a couple of times, reading some dirty magazines, and getting drunk once in a while equal one case of leukemia?"

I almost said I hoped not, because if it did, then I'd have been dead for years. Instead I laughed a little and said, "I hope not, or I'm in for worse."

"Yeah, and I bet there are kids who make us look like angels and they've never been sick a day in their—"

Before he could finish the sentence, a car flew

around a corner near us, its tires screeching, skidding on the loose gravel and dirt left from construction. We both jumped back as it zoomed past. I caught a glimpse of the kids inside; they didn't look old enough to have licenses. One of them had probably "borrowed" his parent's car for a joyride. It was something Chunk and I had done plenty of times before we were old enough to get our licenses.

The car really hadn't come that close to us, but Howie was rattled. "Idiots!" he yelled at the two red taillights disappearing down the road. Then he turned to me. "Let's go back before we get killed."

We walked back, not talking. When we got to the foot of his driveway, I stopped, figuring that I'd head back to my house. Howie looked up at his house and then at me, almost as if he wanted to go to my house instead of his.

"My mother really worries me," Howie said, softly, as if she might be able to hear us all the way at the end of the driveway. "It's like she can't deal with this at all, David."

"Sure she can, Howie. She's just got to, uh . . . adjust to it."

But Howie shook his head. "It goes deeper than that."

"What do you mean?" I asked.

Howie shrugged. "It's hard to explain." He paused and looked up at the house again. "You know how she always kisses me when she leaves the hospital?"

"Yeah?"

"Well, she doesn't really kiss me. All she does is put her lips about half an inch from my head and make a kissing sound."

"So?"

Howie looked straight at me. "She won't touch me anymore," he said. "Ever since I got sick she's been afraid to."

Back at home that night, I went into the den, where my father was half-watching a Clint Eastwood movie on the tube and half-reading a real estate magazine, as if neither was interesting enough to demand his full attention. My father didn't have many interests outside of real estate, our family, and watching pro football in the fall. In that sense he was different from a lot of guys around the Gold Coast who were into sports and sailed or jogged or played tennis or golf.

He'd actually been a star college football halfback in the fifties until a shoulder separation ended his career. And ever since I was a kid he'd had plans for me to be a pro football player. He even bought me my first helmet and set of shoulder pads when I was five. But my mother had vetoed high school football because it was too violent, and I switched to soccer even though my father said it was an "un-American" game. Still, a pro soccer player for a son was better than no pro at all, and despite his lack of interest in soccer, he always made sure he knew exactly how I'd played each game, what the team's standings were, and how my alleged soccer "career" was progressing. He hardly ever asked about school or Rena or anything else I was doing.

"Eight and oh, huh?" he asked, referring to the team's record.

"Yeah."

"Think anyone in the league can beat you?" he asked.

"Anyone can get lucky," I said, affecting the cocky attitude my father liked to see in sports but nowhere else.

It didn't take long to exhaust the topic of soccer, as nothing new had happened since the night before when we'd last talked about it, and we came to an awkward moment when neither of us was sure whether to keep talking or watch television.

"I had dinner at Howie's tonight," I said. "He just got home from the hospital."

"Your mother said you were over there. How is he?"

I told him about how weak Howie had seemed, how uptight his parents were, about the walk we'd taken, and what Howie had said about not understanding why, of all the people in the world, he'd gotten sick. A lot of things I'd been thinking started coming out, and I was surprised to hear myself telling my father about them. "It's not like he stayed out in the cold too long and caught something. What really bothers me is, there's no logical reason why Howie should have leukemia. It's so hard to accept the idea that something like that could just happen."

The real estate magazine on my father's lap was closed and neither of us were aware of who Clint Eastwood was shooting up at the moment. Then the question I'd been wanting to ask all night popped out: "Doesn't it scare you?"

My father didn't answer right away. I guess when you're a father and your son is just a kid, you're supposed to pretend that nothing scares you. It must have taken him a moment to realize we were no longer like that. "Of course it does, David," he said. "It scares everyone."

"What do you do about it?"

My father shrugged and looked back at the television screen, but his eyes weren't following the action. "What can you do about it?" he asked himself. "You just keep going and hope it doesn't happen to you or anyone you love. And maybe once in a while when you're really sore because a deal didn't go through and you wasted a lot of time on it, you stop and think that perhaps you should be glad you're alive and healthy and had the time to waste."

"That helps?" I asked.

My father smiled. "Sometimes."

CHAPTER
TEN

Things with Rena weren't good. It was pretty obvious that she wanted to break up; all I was waiting for was a formal declaration. As we got ready for our ninth game I didn't even want to ask her if she was coming for fear that she'd say no. The problem was, I really felt like I needed some support. We were undefeated and the odds were piling up against us. Winning nine straight is tougher than winning eight straight, and winning eight straight wasn't easy. The team was under a lot of pressure as more and more fans came out to see if we could keep our undefeated record.

About half an hour before the game Coach Lavelle called us together in the locker room. The coach was an English teacher who'd done his graduate work at Oxford in England, where soccer is the national sport. As far as we could tell, that was the only reason why he was the soccer coach, since he knew no more about the game than any of us. Coach Lavelle's forte, actually, was nutrition. His whole approach to sports was that the better you ate, the better you played.

At the locker room meeting Lavelle tossed each of us a Hershey's chocolate bar for extra energy during the game. "Okay, boys, gobble 'em up." Each of us dutifully unwrapped our candy bar and ate it while the coach watched. Then, our energy requirements filled, Lavelle started the pep talk. He put one foot up on the locker room bench and clenched his fists. "Okay, boys, this is the ninth game in our first undefeated season ever, right?"

"Right!" we all yelled.

Lavelle nodded sharply. "Everyone eat a good lunch?"

"Yeah!" shouted everyone who wasn't cracking up.

"Been eating lots of breads, rice, and potatoes?" Lavelle was a proponent of carbohydrate loading.

"Yeah!" everyone shouted again.

"Drink a lot of liquids today?"

"Yeah!"

"All right!" Lavelle clapped his hands together loudly. "What are you gonna do out there today?"

"Puke!" someone yelled. The team immediately collapsed on the benches and locker room floor, laughing and howling. Johnny Jarret laughed so hard he peed in his soccer shorts and had to change while the rest of the team bolted enthusiastically out the door.

Chunk and I jogged together out to the field for warm-ups. It was a warm October day, perfect for a soccer game, and we were amazed at the crowd already in the bleachers waiting for the game to begin. "Soccer fever" was spreading through the school, and we got a loud cheer as we went into our stretches and warm-ups. Jarret joined us later, after changing into a new pair of shorts.

"Hey, Coach," he yelled as he got into the line. "Do I have to drink more liquids?"

It was pretty funny, but no one laughed very long. The game would be starting in a few minutes and we were all too nervous.

It usually took a few moments for the team to get going once the game began. The forwards and midfielders on both sides would kick the ball around, feeling out their opponents and looking for weaknesses. I was still getting settled in the goal when two of their guys suddenly burst out of the midfield with the ball ten feet ahead of them. Jarret came up too fast and they passed the ball behind him, and the next thing I knew, I was diving toward the far end of the goal, but the ball flew beyond my fingers, hit the upright, and ricocheted in. A shot like that was pure luck, but from the bleachers

I heard the biggest crowd of the year groan. Less than one minute into the game and we were behind one—zip.

Johnny Jarret should have stayed in bed that day, or at least he should have gotten back into bed as soon as school was over. Halfway through the first period he tripped a forward on the other team. It was an accident, but the ref called it intentional and ordered a direct penalty kick. I tried a body feint and managed to get three fingers on the ball, but it wasn't enough. Now the score was 2–0, the first time all season that we'd been down by two goals.

To make things worse, Rena was there taking pictures, and since all the action was down at my end of the field, she kept moving around behind the goal. Every time the other team brought the ball down toward our goal—when my concentration on the game should have been at its peak—I couldn't help looking around to see if Rena was watching.

With three minutes left in the half, one of their forwards headed in a corner kick. Three—zip. Not a peep from the crowd. I was beginning to wonder how I could face school the next day when there was a roar from the bleachers and a lot of commotion down at the other end of the field. Billy Lee had retaliated quickly and booted a hard one into the other team's cords. The half ended at 3–1.

Most of us were slow getting back to the bench, not eager to face the crowd in the bleachers behind us.

Lavelle actually had an explanation for our poor play: "You had your chocolate bars late today," he said. "They probably haven't completely digested. If I had to point to one reason why we're behind, I'd say lack of energy."

Chunk turned to me and rolled his eyes. As fullbacks, he and Jarret were having their toughest game of the season. If he was low on energy, it was because he hadn't stopped running for forty minutes. Meanwhile Lavelle passed around cups of Gatorade and each of us had to drink the sweet green liquid warm because the coach said it wasn't good for us to drink cold liquids during strenuous exercise. "They've played a very high-energy game so far," Lavelle said of the other team. "But they may start to tire in the next half. I can see us coming from behind."

"I'm glad someone can," Chunk mumbled, looking up at the crowd in the bleachers. "The biggest crowd of the year," he said in a low voice only a few players around him could hear. "And they gotta pick the day we get whipped."

The ref's whistle blew and it was time to get back on the field. I was walking back toward the goal when I heard someone calling my name. "*Over here, David.*" I looked at the sidelines and saw Howie. There was still a second left before the game resumed and I ran over.

"Boy, did you pick the wrong game," I said.

"Naw, you guys just had a couple of bad breaks," Howie said. "You'll pull it out."

"How'd you get here?" I asked.

"Walked."

"All the way from your house?" It had to be a mile and a half.

Howie grinned. "The chauffeur had the day off."

A ref waved at me and I had to get going. "You gonna stay till the end of the game?" I yelled, running toward the goal.

"Sure," Howie yelled back. "How else do you guys expect to win?"

As play resumed, Chunk came over and stood near the goal. He could do that sometimes when the ball was at the other end of the field. "Who's that?" he asked.

"Howie, the kid with leukemia," I said. "He says we're gonna win."

Chunk shook his head disdainfully. "Him and Lavelle."

There was a shout and we saw that the ball was bouncing down the field toward us, chased by a pack of players fighting for control. Chunk ran up the field to stop the attack. Usually a fullback's job would be to intercept the ball and pass it to a midfielder who would take it back across midfield, but

Chunk was an impulsive player. Instead of trapping the ball, he booted a line drive straight across the field. The move surprised everyone, including one of our wingers who suddenly found the ball rolling to his feet. He quickly dribbled down the sideline and crossed it to Billy, right in front of the other team's goal. It was a perfect cross, and Billy followed it with a perfect shot. Suddenly the crowd in the bleachers was on its feet, cheering. The score was 3–2. We were only one goal behind.

Ten minutes later one of our forwards made the third goal and tied the game. The bleachers shook with ecstatic fans, but when I looked across at Howie, he was just standing there smiling at me. The walk from his house must have taken a lot out of him, and he probably didn't have the energy to do somersaults, but he didn't have to let me know he was rooting.

We held the other team scoreless and the second half ended in a tie. Then, instead of being exhausted after eighty minutes of intensive play, we stampeded into sudden-death overtime like a herd of wild buffalo juiced on Hershey bars and Gatorade. The other team never had a chance. Our guys had a free-for-all on their goal until Billy kicked one in. The next thing I knew, everyone was cheering and jumping up and down. You would have thought we'd just won the World Cup.

A lot of people ran out onto the field to congratulate the players. Players were hugging players, fans were hugging players, some fans were even hugging other fans, although I wasn't sure why. Rena was on the field, taking pictures of Billy, who'd been hoisted up on the shoulders of some guys. As usual he deserved it. He'd scored three of our four goals. I looked for Howie and saw him waiting on the sidelines. He probably felt a little shy about joining all the strangers on the field, so I got my warm-ups from the bench and went over to him.

"Good game," he said.

"Yeah." We started walking back toward the gym and I put my arm across his shoulders. I don't know why, it was a pretty corny thing to do, but I felt like doing it just the same. "So how are you feeling?"

"Pretty good," Howie said. "Still get tired sometimes, but other than that, okay."

After home games the team usually went to the local Friendly's for a victory dinner. "You want to come with us?" I asked.

Howie said he couldn't go.

"Well, you want to wait? I'll get you a ride home," I said. There was a school rule that guys not on the team weren't allowed in the locker room after a game, because the coaches were afraid sports equipment would be stolen. So I told Howie to wait in the hall while I showered and dressed.

Chunk was into his postgame untaping ceremony when I sat down next to him in the locker room. "You going to Friendly's?" I asked.

"Yeah."

"Could you drop Howie off at his house on the way? He needs a ride home."

"It's only a two-seater," Chunk said. He had an MGB.

"I'll get a ride with someone else."

A pained look appeared on Chunk's face. "I don't want to take him alone."

This surprised me. "It's only for a couple of minutes, and it's on the way," I said. "I didn't think it would be a big deal or anything, Chunk."

Chunk shrugged and didn't say anything. He finished removing the tape, pulled off his shorts and jock, and grabbed a towel, like he was heading toward the showers.

"You won't take him?" I asked.

Chunk looked down at the locker room floor. "Okay, but you come too. We'll squeeze it." He turned around and headed for the shower room before I could say thanks.

There was a bunch of friends and girl friends of guys on the team waiting outside the locker room when Chunk and I came out. I was secretly hoping Rena would be there too, but she wasn't. Chunk hadn't said a word to me while we dressed and I knew he was mad, but what could I do? We found

Howie standing alone a little ways down the corridor. He looked glad to see us.

"Howie, this is Chunk," I said. "Chunk, Howie." Chunk sort of waved at Howie. He didn't try to shake his hand.

"I hope it's not out of the way," Howie said.

Chunk shook his head and we walked out to the parking lot. The top was down on the MGB and Chunk asked Howie if he wanted him to put it up. "Are you kidding?" Howie said. He and Chunk got into the seats and I scrunched down in the space behind them.

The road from school was narrow and winding and Chunk liked to take it fast, downshifting into the curves, skidding a little as we went around, and then accelerating out of them. Howie held on to the dashboard, and I braced myself against the seats. After we went through the second curb, Howie looked back at me, the smile on his face reaching from cheek to cheek.

A few minutes later we made the turn into Cooper's Neck Estates.

"You better leave me here," Howie said when we were still a couple of doors from his house. Chunk slowed down and stopped. "If my mother sees me come home in a sports car, she'll have a fit," Howie said, getting out. "But that was great. Thanks a lot, Chunk."

"Sure." Chunk now acted like it was nothing.

Howie turned to me. "See you soon, okay?"

"Yeah, Howie." I climbed into the front seat.

Chunk pulled a fast U-turn, tires squealing and skidding, and we zoomed out of Cooper's Neck Estates. He was quiet the rest of the way to Friendly's, but when we got out of the car he said, "You satisfied?"

"Come on, Chunk, it wasn't that bad," I said, slapping him on the back.

But Chunk just shoved his hands into his pockets and didn't say a thing.

CHAPTER
ELEVEN

The next day I found a large manila envelope in my locker. Inside it was a big black-and-white photograph of Howie and me, my arm around his shoulders, walking away from the soccer field. Rena must have taken it after the game the day before. It was a really good picture and reflected a feeling of friendship, although I didn't think I could show it to any friends without getting kidded about being gay or something.

I decided to take it home and frame it and maybe even ask Rena to make another copy for Howie. It was a really nice gesture on Rena's part. In fact, it was amazing how nice she could be sometimes. For days I'd been thinking she wanted to break up, and in the meantime she'd made this beautiful photo for me.

But then I noticed the note at the bottom of the envelope. It was in Rena's handwriting:

Dear David,

I know I should be saying this in person, but I can't bring myself to do it. I don't think we should see each other anymore. I used to think you were different from the rest. You wanted to do something daring and out of the ordinary, and I admired you for that. But now it turns out that you just want to follow the crowd and do what's safe and easy. I'm sorry, but I don't have much respect for that. I think it's sad because in some ways I still like you very much, but sometimes we have to make cerebral decisions.

—Rena

P.S. As a parting gesture, I thought you'd like this picture.

I went straight to the darkroom. It was smoky inside, and too dark to see. But across the room I saw the dull red ember of a burning cigarette.

"Rena?"

She didn't answer.

"Rena, I know you're there," I said.

Still no answer.

"Okay," I said angrily, "don't talk. I've plenty to say anyway and the first thing is, what kind of crap is this about cerebral decisions? That's the kind of bull I can't stand and you know it. You've got this whole thing backward, Rena. A jock who wants to grow up and be a professional athlete

94

isn't daring, it's typical. Come on, Rena, I could get scholarships to half a dozen schools. What's so daring about that? But giving up a scholarship for something I really think is important is sort of risky. If I don't make it to med school, I'll blow the whole thing. I thought you'd realize that."

I paused for a second to see if Rena felt like talking yet. But the red ember just continued to glow silently in the dark. "Well, I guess I was wrong, Rena, but I'd still like to know why you want to break up. Excuse my deficiencies in the English language, but I don't think a cerebral decision is a clear enough explanation, and I do think I deserve to know."

Apparently Rena didn't feel I deserved an answer. I was just about to tell her what a chicken she was when the red ember made a funny zigzag movement. Something about it struck me as odd and I reached over and flicked on the safelight switch. The room instantly brightened and I found myself facing not one, but two people.

And neither was Rena. They were two guys, juniors.

Oh, crap.

"What are you doing here?" I yelled, mostly because I was embarrassed.

One of the kids looked really scared. "Just looking for a place to grab a butt," he stammered.

His friend was cooler. "Sorry about your girl friend," he said, smiling.

I gave him the finger and left.

The automotive shop was just down the hall from the darkroom. Our high school gave one course on auto mechanics, which was basically a lesson on tuning European sports cars. It was split evenly between males and females and was the only class Chunk never missed.

He saw me at the doorway and nodded as if he knew what I was going to say. Even though class was in session, I stepped into the shop and stood next to a greasy car engine hanging in the air from a hoist. Chunk joined me there. "Sara told me," he whispered.

"How come I only found out five minutes ago?" I whispered back.

Chunk looked pretty discouraged. "Listen, the only reason I know is because Sara broke up with me last night."

I stared at him. "You mean they decided *together*?" I must have said it too loudly because half the class turned and looked at us. Someone even giggled.

Chunk shrugged. "What did Rena say?"

"She didn't say anything," I whispered. "She left me a note saying that it was a cerebral decision."

"What's that, French?"

"No, it means it was an intellectual decision instead of an emotional one."

"You guys were together for a long time."

"Almost a year."

Chunk looked back at the class. There wasn't much more to say about it. Some of the class was still looking at us. "Listen, you want to go to the city Friday night? I know this girl from the Vineyard. She goes to some private school. I could ask her if she has a friend."

"Chunk, you just broke up with Sara last night."

Chunk fidgeted a little. "So what do you want me to do? Go into mourning?"

I left the shop and after asking around a little more, found out that Rena had left school for the day. That made me mad. She couldn't even face me, and what was worse was that she left me to face all the kids at school who seemed to know more about our breaking up than I did. News that the captain and goalie of the soccer team had been collectively dumped crossed the school faster than the flu the day before Christmas vacation. I knew because everywhere I went kids stared at me. What did they expect *me* to do? *Go into mourning?*

After practice I called Rena's house, but her mother answered and said she was at Sara's. So I called there.

"Hello?"

"Hi, Sara, it's David. Can I speak to Rena?"

"Oh—uh—wait a minute, David. I'll see if she wants to speak to you." She got off, but I already knew Rena wouldn't talk to me.

"David?" It was Sara again.

"Where's Rena?"

"She doesn't want to talk to you."

"Sara, did it ever strike you how silly and immature it is for two girls to get together and decide to dump their boyfriends?"

"That's not how it occurred," Sara replied calmly. "We've both been unhappy tied down."

That was too much. "Sure, Sara," I practically yelled into the phone. "I bet it's been tough. After all, you've been tied down to Chunk for at least two weeks."

"You're so rude, David," Sara said.

"And you're such an immature little phony!" I shouted. But she'd already hung up.

CHAPTER
TWELVE

By the end of October colleges and universities from as far away as California and Texas had flown Chunk and Billy to their campuses for visits and interviews. Weeks before, Coach Lavelle had asked me why I wasn't accepting similar invitations, and I'd told him about my plans for pre-med. The coach was pretty cool about it. He said he was disappointed, but he respected my decision and offered to write recommendations to Tufts and Columbia and the other schools where I'd applied.

I'd applied to just about every college with a good pre-med program that I thought I had a chance at and begged most of them to wait for my mid-year grades before making a decision. My three-year average wasn't so hot, but I hoped that if I pulled a couple of A's by Christmas, I could prove I was serious.

At home I avoided the whole issue, hoping my

father might forget about college soccer teams and scholarships. Fat chance. Finally, at dinner one night he asked me if I planned to visit Hartwick College, a major soccer school, in Upstate New York.

My mother quickly got up from the table. "I'll go make some coffee," she said, heading for the kitchen. Chicken, I thought.

I figured it was best to get it all out at once: "I'm not applying to any of the schools that invited me, Dad."

My father didn't respond right away. I guess he was considering the implications of what I'd said. "You're not going to accept a scholarship?" he asked.

I tried to avoid his eyes. "I want to go to a school with a good pre-med program."

"Pre-med?" he asked, surprised.

It must have sounded like it came straight out of left field. I realized that keeping the whole pre-med thing a secret from him for so long probably wasn't a real smart idea. "Dad, do you know why I took biology and psych in summer school?" I noticed my mother was standing quietly in the doorway, watching us.

"Well, I—uh—" My father looked up at my mother. "Did you know about this?" he asked.

She nodded.

"I needed the grades to get into a college with a

good pre-med program," I said. "I didn't tell you before because I wanted to first make sure that it was what I wanted to do."

My father stared at me, disbelieving. "And you think you're sure now?" he asked. I couldn't expect him to be thrilled. After all, I'd just told him I wanted to spend about thirty thousand dollars of his money on a college education I could have gotten free. "Can't you do pre-med at a college that gives you a scholarship?"

"I don't want to be responsible to a team, Dad. It's hard enough to get good grades for med school without feeling obligated to practice every day and travel to every away game. Besides, the schools I think I should apply to aren't the ones offering the scholarships."

"But you'll join a soccer team wherever you go," he said.

"I might, or I might just play intramural," I said. "The things is, I'm no longer heading in the same direction, Dad. College, the NCAA's, the Olympics, the pros, forget it. I want to be a doctor, not a soccer player."

My father still didn't seem convinced. He looked again at my mother. "Isn't it more important," she asked, "that he get the best education he can and not simply the cheapest?"

My father sighed and I winked at my mother. She'd scored an important point. Now my father looked from her to me. Not only was the money bothering him, I imagined, but now it was no longer "my son, the pro athlete."

"You didn't think I'd understand?" he asked.

"Do you?" I asked.

My father frowned. "You're right. I think it's ludicrous."

I left my parents in the dining room to talk and went into my room to do my homework. But I couldn't concentrate.

Of course my father must have been pissed. For more than a year I'd led him to believe that I'd take a scholarship, go to college, and then to the pros. Not that I really needed a scholarship—although at $24,000 to $30,000 a pop for college, it didn't hurt—but players who got them usually got better coaching and more playing time than those who didn't. Even if a nonscholarship player was as good as a scholarship player, the scholarship meant status, reputation, seriousness. And if you were working toward the pros, those things counted.

But if playing for the pros was what I wanted to do, why even bother with college? Why not just go straight from high school into the pros? Because maybe, deep down, I know that there was a chance I wouldn't make it to the pros. Sure, I was a good high school player and probably I'd be a good college player, but that didn't mean anything in the pros, where you not only competed against the best players in the United States but against the best players from Europe, South America, and Central America as well. Watching Billy Lee that fall, I began to realize what you needed to get to the pros. It wasn't only natural ability and reflexes, it wasn't just hours of practice. You had to be a fanatic. I loved to play soccer, but I was no fanatic. There were other things in life that I thought were more important.

Later that evening my father came in and sat down on my bed. For a while he didn't say anything, he just looked at the posters of Pelé and Giorgio Chinaglia and other soccer stars I had tacked up on my walls. There were also a couple of trophies I'd won in summer league tournaments on the shelf. But his eyes stopped at the photo of Howie and me that I'd hung in a plastic frame. He stood up and took a closer look at it. "Who's this?"

"Howie Jamison."

He stared at the picture for a while and then turned to me. "Did he have anything to do with this decision?"

I nodded, but I couldn't think of how to explain it.

My father rubbed his hands together. "But you decided to go to summer school before you met him."

"Yeah," I said. "Knowing Howie just sort of helped me focus on it better."

My father stepped back to the bed and sat down

again. "Well, David, I'll be honest with you. I'm disappointed. I thought you'd go all the way with soccer. And I admit that the money's a factor. I was looking forward to buying a place in Maine."

If he had stopped there, I might have changed my mind and taken a scholarship, but he kept talking about a medical degree and how it meant grinding through another eight to ten years of school and how the real estate market was really tight these days and I'd probably have to take some college loans. Then he talked about a friend of his in college who'd become a doctor and how tough it was working nights as an intern, having to pay back all those loans, always being on call and worrying about patients. He even mentioned the increase in malpractice suits against doctors and how expensive malpractice insurance was.

Then he talked about how great it would be as a professional athlete and how you could make a lot of money, travel all over the world meeting interesting people, and make television commercials and endorse products. And when you retired, you could open a soccer camp and only work four months a year.

I just kept nodding. It amused me a little that he did not even consider the possibility that I might not make the pros. The more he talked, the more I realized that his disappointment wasn't for me, but for him. Now he wasn't going to be the father of a pro soccer player. For the second time in his life he'd failed to make it in pro sports. I felt kind of bad for him.

Finally he stopped talking. "You are certain you won't accept a scholarship?"

"Pretty much, yeah."

My father stood up. "I just don't want you to wind up regretting that you missed this opportunity."

"I appreciate that, Dad."

My father stopped at the door and looked back at me. "See if you can get the lawn cut this weekend. If I'm going to help put you through another eight years of school, it's the least you could do." But as he said it he smiled a little.

CHAPTER
THIRTEEN

The team continued undefeated, and we were virtually assured of a spot in the sectional tournament, which preceded the regional playoffs, which preceded the state championships. The team spirit was tense—we'd already come a long way and yet it seemed like we had an even longer way to go. Tempers grew brittle and for the first time in six years there were arguments in the locker room and nasty remarks on the field when a player made a mistake.

Finally, after the game that clinched us a place in the sectionals, Chunk announced that he was throwing a party to celebrate. Confidentially, he told me that Coach Lavelle had not only suggested the party, but was kicking in $150 for food and refreshments. We agreed that while the coach might not know much about soccer, he was pretty good at handling a team.

Howie had just gotten out of the hospital after five days of maintenance therapy and I decided to ask him to come to the party too. I hadn't seen him since he'd come home, but we'd talked on the phone and he sounded pretty bummed out. I hoped the party would cheer him up.

"I don't know, David," Howie said when I called to invite him.

"Are you feeling okay?" I asked.

"Yeah, about the same lately."

"Would the doctors let you?"

"As long as I took it easy."

"So come on. When was the last time you went to a party?"

There was a pause on the phone. Then Howie said, "About two million years ago."

"Then you gotta come."

"I don't know, David."

"You can tell your parents it's chaperoned." Technically it would be. Mrs. Lowell would probably lock herself in her bedroom and keep the television on loud all night.

"It's not that, David."

"So what could it be?" I asked. "Look, I'll pick you up at eight, and I promise to have you home by eleven-thirty, okay?"

"It's kind of weird, David," Howie said.

"No excuses," I said. "See you Friday."

When I arrived at Howie's house that Friday,

Mrs. Jamison met me at the door. "David, please don't take Howie to the party." She spoke in a low voice so that Howie wouldn't hear.

"Is something wrong?" I asked.

Mrs. Jamison was about to explain when Howie appeared in the living room wearing a new pair of jeans and a beige crew neck sweater. He was dressed like a true Gold Coaster, except for the wool ski cap pulled down around his ears.

"Hi, David." He had a funny grin on his face.

Mrs. Jamison stared at her son. "Howie," she said, "you look ridiculous in that hat."

The grin disappeared from Howie's face.

"What's going on?" I asked.

"Look, David." Howie pulled off the ski hat. Underneath he was completely bald.

"They'll make fun of him," Mrs. Jamison said.

Howie looked at me. "Tell me the truth, David. Do you think they will?"

It took me a moment to recover from the surprise of seeing him bald. But the way he asked I knew he really wanted to go to the party. He'd been cooped up in the house and the hospital for almost two months, and hair or no hair, he needed to get out. "No one will make fun of him, Mrs. Jamison," I said. "They're nice kids, and they know Howie's been sick. They wouldn't dare pick on him."

"They'll stare at him," Mrs. Jamison said.

"Yes, they probably will," I said. "But they'll stop staring after a while. If someone came with their arm or leg in a cast, they'd stare at him too."

Mrs. Jamison shook her head. "I think it's a very bad idea."

I felt pretty uncomfortable being caught in the middle between Howie and his mother, but I was certain the problem was her being overprotective and not Howie's bald head.

"I really want to go, Mom," Howie said. "Even if they stare at me, at least it's something to do."

"You'd like being stared at?" his mother asked.

"Well . . ." Howie grinned again. "By the right girl, sure."

"We'll be back early," I said.

Mrs. Jamison looked at me resentfully and I had a feeling I'd just made an enemy. It wasn't fair. I wished she'd understand, but I knew she wouldn't. Some people are like that. If you don't agree with them, you're automatically the bad guy.

"The doctor said you mustn't drink," she said to Howie.

"I won't," Howie said.

Mrs. Jamison didn't give in easily. "Howie . . . please."

What a mess. Howie glanced at me and I was almost certain he'd relent. How could you refuse when she sounded so distraught? But Howie shook his head. Suddenly Mrs. Jamison's face changed from soft to hard. "Howie," she said, her ire rising, "you're a foolish boy. And"—she turned and stared venomously at me—"you have foolish friends." Then she went into the kitchen and slammed the door behind her.

Howie looked at me, his lips pinched tightly. Somehow he'd known there'd be no tears and no falling apart. Behind Mrs. Jamison's mask of fragile femininity was the toughness of a state trooper.

From the moment Howie got into the car he was in the best mood I'd seen him in since he'd gotten sick. On the way to Chunk's we stopped at a traffic light and a man in the car next to us stared at him. Howie rolled down the window. "Excuse me, sir," he yelled, "but do you know where I can get a cheap toupee?"

The man gasped and quickly drove away.

Chunk's place was actually a small estate. His father was a stock broker on Wall Street, and every morning a rented limousine picked him up and took him to the city. Mr. Lowell used to have the limo to himself, but after the price of gas went up he started sharing it with two other guys who worked in the stock market. It must have been a tough sacrifice.

The Lowells' house was painted yellow and looked like a French chateau. In the summer Mrs. Lowell made it look really pretty with window boxes of flowers and green-striped awnings. They had a tennis court and a swimming pool in the backyard and a couple of acres of woods where Chunk and I used to play as kids.

When we got there, the party had already started and everyone was out back on the terrace around the swimming pool. The pool was covered with a plastic tarp. It was too cold to go swimming, and most of the guests were wearing sweaters or jackets. The whole backyard was lit with outdoor lights that cast deep shadows through the trees. Mrs. Jamison was right about one thing—as soon as Howie and I stepped through the shadows, the guys nearest us turned and stared.

"Have no fear," Howie announced. "I bear gifts from the planet Xenon."

Those who heard him scowled. I had a feeling Howie was overestimating their collective sense of humor. Then Chunk ambled up, beer in hand, wearing his cowboy hat and a fringed suede jacket. Howie had no wisecracks for him. "The treatment made my hair fall out," he said.

Chunk nodded. I knew he was trying not to stare, but it was hard to resist. If any of us had ever wondered what it would be like to be bald at seventeen, here was the answer.

"You want a beer or something?" Chunk asked.

"Got any pop?"

"Sure." Chunk pointed to a large ice-filled cooler near the pool. "Help yourself."

While Howie got a soda, Chunk asked me how he was feeling.

"Okay, I guess," I said. "All I know is that he's still under treatment."

"I wonder how he feels about losing his hair," Chunk said.

"I guess he doesn't have much choice."

Howie returned with a can of soda for himself and two cans of beer, for Chunk and me.

"Thanks, Howie."

"You bet." Howie raised his can. "Here's to the team and the championship this year."

"Hey, all right!" We took deep gulps.

"Think you'll come to our next game?" Chunk asked.

"If I can," Howie said. "The doctors say I may even be able to go back to school."

We toasted again.

"It's just that with the chemotherapy and everything, I'll still wind up missing a lot," Howie said. "Those treatments can really run you down."

"I know," Chunk said, commiserating. "My aunt went through them."

"She did!?" Howie asked excitedly. "She had chemotherapy?"

"Uh, yeah," Chunk said.

"For what?" Howie asked.

I glanced nervously at Chunk, hoping he wouldn't say the wrong thing. After all, his aunt hadn't made it. "Cancer of the uterus," Chunk said.

"How long'd she have it?" Howie wanted to know.

"About two years," Chunk said.

"How's she doing now?" Howie asked. I felt my stomach tighten.

"She's doing fine, Howie," Chunk lied.

Howie smiled. "Boy, that's good to hear," he said. "The one thing that really gets you is how there's nobody else you know who's been through the same thing. Every time I hear about someone who's had chemotherapy, it makes me feel better. Like I'm not the only person in the world who's ever gone through it."

Chunk and I stood there nodding anxiously.

"Uh, listen," Chunk said, "it's getting kind of cold out here. You think I should move the party inside?"

"Yes," I said, feeling relieved that we were off the subject of his aunt. "Can I take Howie on a tour?"

"Sure, just don't go upstairs," Chunk said. "My mother's probably in her nightgown."

Without going upstairs I was able to show Howie the living room, dining room, kitchen, study, den, greenhouse, and a couple of other rooms whose purpose was a mystery. Not that any of this impressed Howie. It wasn't until we got downstairs to the big basement recreation room where Chunk moved the party that Howie was impressed.

"A pinball machine?" he said, seeing the one Chunk had in the corner of the room. "Does it work?"

"Sure."

Howie couldn't get over the idea that Chunk had his own pinball machine. "A Bally Captain Fantastic!" He fawned over the machine like it was a piece of rare art. A second later he was reaching into his pocket.

"Don't bother," I said, pointing to a bowl filled with slugs on a shelf near the machine. With the first ball Howie ran up a score of 220,000 points and quickly attracted three or four other pinball players who put in their challenges. For the first time that evening the people around Howie weren't staring at his head. Instead, they were staring through the glass at the silver ball that Howie seemed to keep in play endlessly.

By now the party was going full tilt in the rec room. Everyone was dancing and drinking and the smell of grass was heavy in the air. Howie was preoccupied with pinball, so I wandered over to Billy Lee and some of the soccer players.

"Is that the kid who has cancer?" someone asked.

"Yeah, but he's doing okay," I said quickly.

"What happened to his hair?" Johnny Jarret asked.

"Go ask him," I said. I really didn't feel like being Howie's official spokesman for the evening.

"Don't be a nerd, David."

I sighed. Giving up the spokesman job wasn't going to be easy. I explained about Howie's treatments.

"You hear about Billy?" Johnny asked when I'd finished.

I looked at Billy, who was quiet as usual. Only an uncharacteristically broad smile gave him away. "Which school?" I asked.

"Saint Louis. Four years, all expenses," Billy said.

"And maybe a little pull for the '84 Olympics," Johnny added for him.

"How's that?"

Billy tried to shrug it off. I think he was blushing, but it was too dark to tell. "Just that the Saint Louis coach is on the Olympic Soccer Committee," he said. "But that doesn't mean anything."

"Sure it doesn't," Johnny cracked.

I looked at Billy. So there it was, a four-year paid scholarship plus a shot at the Olympics. It was real. Suddenly I began to regret a little. Maybe my father was right—maybe it was too good an opportunity to pass up.

Chunk appeared across the room with two girls I didn't recognize. But I had a feeling that one of them was the girl Chunk knew from the city and the other girl had been brought along to meet a certain friend of Chunk's who had recently been dumped by Rena Steuben. Sure enough, Chunk waved me over. I went, thinking, Thanks for warning me ahead of time, Chunk. But he probably knew I never would have gone along with the blind date if I'd had a choice.

Introductions were made. They were Katie and Carol, both blond, both wearing Seven Sisters sweaters, corduroy jeans, and clogs—preppy training uniforms. Carol was taller than Katie and slightly better looking, although they were both pretty. Carol was with Chunk, which meant that by design and default Katie was with me. For a moment I considered the possibilities, but then Katie asked what position I played on the soccer team and I realized I really didn't want to be paired up with anyone new and have to start explaining all the things that Rena already understood.

Still, mostly for Chunk's sake, I followed the unwritten law of double-dating and resigned myself to entertaining Katie so that he could be alone with Carol. Someone turned up the music and it got so noisy and smoky in the rec room that I suggested to Katie that we get our jackets and go back outside. She cautiously agreed, probably wondering what moves I was going to put on her. As we went out the door to the backyard I caught Chunk's eye and he winked. Boy, I thought, do you have the wrong idea.

We sat on some chaises. In the dark shadows outside the lighted area around the pool we heard someone giggling. Katie smiled at me nervously. It was chilly, but she didn't seem to mind and we started talking about the school she went to in New York—I think she said Dalton—and what it was like. I kept expecting her to light a cigarette, since no conversation with Rena was complete without one. Katie said she lived on East 57th Street with her parents and planned to major in English in college. I only half heard her as I thought back to the days Rena and I had spent together that summer; Rena with her camera on a tripod near the edge of the pond; Rena at the Museum of Modern Art in the city, looking at photography exhibits; Rena lying naked on a deep-blue carpet upstairs at Sara's house one afternoon while everyone else was out at the beach swimming.

"David?" Katie said.

"Uh, yeah?"

She handed me an empty glass. "Would you get me some more wine?"

"Sure."

I went back inside, noticing that the party had changed. The music was softer and the dancing was closer. A couple was making out in the dark and some guys were sitting in a circle, passing a joint. Howie was still playing pinball. I refilled Katie's glass, picked up a beer, and stopped by the pinball machine.

"How're you doing?"

"Fantastic," he said. I noticed that a girl named Sherry from my class was watching him play. She wasn't much of a looker, but she was a good kid and a pal to a lot of the jocks.

"You know, we probably ought to leave pretty soon," I said.

Lights were flashing and buzzers were buzzing all over the pinball machine. "No way," Howie said. "This is the best time I've had since I moved up here."

"It's early, David," Sherry said. "Don't be a flake. Howie's teaching me how to play."

"Yeah." Howie held up his wristwatch. "It's not even tomorrow yet." He took a gulp of soda from a paper cup and teetered slightly, leading me to suspect that his cups of Coke were spiked with something.

"Listen, Howie," I said. "I promised your mother I'd bring you home early and sober. You may have lost your hair, but if I bring you home late *and* drunk, I'll probably lose my head."

"Which would be an improvement," Sherry said.

But Howie understood, somewhat. "We don't have to go yet, do we?" he asked, looking back at Sherry for a second.

I sighed. It wouldn't be so bad if we were back by midnight. Besides, here I was getting Howie away from his overprotective mother and being overprotective myself. "What about this?" I pointed to the Coke.

"Last one." Howie gulped it down, crumpled the cup in his hand, and grinned at me sheepishly.

"That was great, Howie," I said, heavy on the sarcasm.

Meanwhile, Sherry slipped another slug into the pinball machine. "How do you keep it from going in the hole, Howie?" she asked, taking over the flippers. Howie spun around. "Here, use a little body English. . . ."

I left Howie and his body English and went back outside. Katie thanked me for the wine and I sat down at the foot of her chaise. It was a clear night and the sky was full of stars.

"It's nice out," Katie said.

"Yeah."

"I'll bet you used to bring your girl friend here."

Great, I thought, now what am I supposed to say?

"I wouldn't have brought it up," Katie said, "except that you seem so preoccupied, and Carol told me you'd just broken up. Was it serious?"

I winced. "Guess my end of it was."

"Sorry." She sighed.

"Look, don't let me keep you out here," I said, feeling embarrassed. Of course this was all Chunk's fault. Damn Chunk.

Katie shook her head. "I'd just as soon be out here," she said. "Do you feel like talking about her?"

"About my girl friend?" I asked, incredulous.

"Uh-huh."

As a matter of fact, I did feel like talking about Rena. So why not talk to Katie? The only other people I could have talked to were Chunk, who didn't seem very sympathetic, and Rena, who, under the present circumstances, had sort of canceled herself out. Even though she was a stranger, Katie seemed interested, and at least I wouldn't have to worry about her blabbing my secrets all over school. So I told her how I felt about Rena, and some of the things I said even surprised me. Like, that Rena could be selfish and spoiled and self-centered, but also that I admired and respected her intelligence. And how sometimes in private she was surprisingly gentle, loving, and passionate. I also said how proud I was that she was a good photographer and not just a lot of talk, like Robert Tuckel, who called himself an artist, but probably couldn't even paint by numbers. I even admitted how much I missed Rena. I guess I talked about her for quite a while.

"You want me to pay you twenty bucks for this session or something?" I asked, sort of as a joke.

Katie laughed. "I'd be rich if I charged for that, David," she said. "It happens to me all the time."

"Oh, yeah? Strangers just come up to you in the street and start blabbing?"

"Not exactly. But do you want to know what I think?"

"What?"

"I think Rena really blew it."

"How come?"

"Because you really love her."

"You think so?" I said. "I wasn't sure, I've never been in love before."

Katie smiled. "Neither have I, David, but I've heard about it from enough people to know."

Neither of us said anything for a few moments. Katie's analysis didn't make me feel any better. In fact, it made me feel worse. Finally, I stood up and said, "A lot of good it does me now." My legs felt stiff, as if I'd been sitting in the cold for a long time. Could I have been? "What time is it?"

"A quarter past one," Katie said.

"Oh, no— I gotta go."

Howie wasn't in the rec room. No one seemed to know where he'd gone, although one guy said that if I found him, he wanted a rematch in pinball. I ran upstairs looking for Chunk, but as I crossed the living room I noticed someone curled up on a couch.

"Howie, wake up." I shook him on the shoulder.

"Hmm . . ." Howie shrugged and nestled more deeply into the couch.

"Come on, Howie, we're late."

"Hmm. Great party," Howie mumbled. "Great."

"Come on, baldy." I shook him.

Howie hid his head under a pillow. "Go ahead without me," he said.

"I can't go anywhere without you, now come

on," I said, pulling his arm. Howie allowed himself to be pulled up to a sitting position, but he sat there with his head bent and eyes closed, as if he were asleep sitting up.

"I'm so tired." He yawned.

I got Howie out to the car, but he didn't seem to quite wake up. I'd never seen anyone so tired, and I was scared that something was wrong. He was asleep again the moment he sat down in the car seat.

It seemed like every light in the Jamison house was on. Even before I parked the car the front door opened and Mr. Jamison came out. Behind him I saw Mrs. Jamison standing in the doorway. "Is he all right, Edward?" she asked.

Mr. Jamison looked at Howie in the front seat and then at me. He was really mad. "He's sound asleep," I said.

Mr. Jamison nodded and looked back at his wife. "He's all right," he said.

I watched while he opened the car door and tried to get Howie out of the car. "You better give me a hand," he said. Together we half walked and half carried Howie into the house and upstairs to his bedroom. As we were putting him down on the bed I suddenly realized that they probably thought he was dead-drunk.

Mrs. Jamison glared at me as I went back downstairs. Mr. Jamison followed me out to the car. "How much did he have to drink, David?" he asked, barely holding in his anger.

"Not that much," I said meekly.

Mr. Jamison nodded, his lips pressed together. He turned without saying a word and walked back into the house.

It was almost 2:00 A.M. when I got home. There was a light on in my house also and I found my mother, in her bathrobe, waiting for me. "Is Howie all right?" she asked as I stepped into the house.

"Yeah, just a little tired, that's all." I meant to shrug it off, but the whole episode with his parents had really depressed me.

My mother looked concerned. "Are you sure? The Jamisons called here three times tonight in a panic. You knew they'd be worried if he stayed out late, didn't you?"

"Yeah," I said. "It's my fault. First he didn't want to leave, and then I met someone and I forgot what time it was. But he's okay, Mom. His parents think he got drunk, but he's just pooped, that's all."

"You mustn't forget that he's a very sick boy, David," my mother said, following me down the hall to the bathroom. "The Jamisons were ready to call the police."

"I'm sorry, Mom, I blew it." I stopped at the bathroom door and waited to see if she had anything more to say, but she only nodded slowly. I guess she could see that I was bummed out by the whole thing. "See you in the morning." I closed the door.

I brushed my teeth, wondering if Howie really had gotten drunk. He had had enough time while I was outside with Katie, but he'd told me he wouldn't drink any more. I thought about calling Sherry to ask her, but it was too late. What if Howie woke up the next morning with a bad hangover? The Jamisons would have my head. All I'd meant was for Howie to get out and have a good time. Now what a mess.

I retraced the party in my mind, trying to recall any clues that Howie had gotten drunk. But my thoughts went back to Katie and stopped, remembering what she'd said. *"You really love her."* In the excitement about Howie I'd forgotten. Maybe Katie was right, but so what? It only made me feel worse. What did it matter if I did love Rena? Would it change her mind if I told her I loved her? —showed up at her door the next morning with a bouquet of roses? If anyone was a sucker for romance, it was me, not her.

What *did* matter to her? I wondered. What could change her mind? I really didn't know. I just wished she loved me, and I wished Howie's parents weren't so pissed. Suddenly my skull felt tight and hot and my arms and legs tingled. Everything started buzzing, and I thought for a second that I might puke. I leaned against the edge of the sink until the sensation went away, leaving me feeling lonelier than I'd ever felt before.

When I opened the bathroom door again, someone was standing out in the hall. I jumped. "Aw, Mom, you scared me."

"Did you say you met someone?" she asked. "What about Rena?"

"Mom, have you been standing here since I closed the door?" I asked.

"Are you avoiding my question?" she asked.

I switched off the bathroom light and stepped around her, quickly heading for my room.

"David?" she called behind me, but I didn't turn around. There was no way I was going to let my mother see me cry.

I waited until eleven the next morning to call Howie's. Mrs. Jamison answered the phone and said he was still sleeping. She added that they had called the doctor that morning and he'd said Howie was probably all right.

"I'm really sorry, Mrs. Jamison," I said. "I went outside and forgot what time it was. Howie fell asleep on a couch. I really don't think he got drunk or anything."

"That's all right, David," Mrs. Jamison said. She sounded very cool and distant, and I could tell that as far as she was concerned, I was now one of the enemy. She probably figured Chunk's party was some kind of orgy and that I'd been out in the bushes all night. Not only was I certain that Howie's parents would put a leash around his neck from now on, but I was afraid he might be forbidden to see me as well.

My suspicions weren't altogether unfounded, as I learned a few hours later when Howie called back. "They thought I was drunk," he said.

"Yeah, I know."

"It took me an hour just to convince them I wasn't."

"How'd you do it?"

"I told them they could call up Chunk's mother and ask her how much rum was left in the bottle. All I had was a couple of rum and Cokes."

"They wouldn't do it, huh?"

"Are you serious?" Howie asked. "Can you see my mother calling up Chunk's mother? 'Hello, Mrs. Chunk? This is Howie Jamison's mother calling. Would you mind checking the level of the rum bottle in your basement liquor cabinet for me? Thank you.'"

"So what did they say?"

"They couldn't believe Chunk's parents would let him have a party with alcohol. It's a good thing they don't know about the pot. My mother's convinced you're all straight out of Sodom and Gomorrah."

"What are they going to do?" I asked.

"They already did it," Howie said. "The sentence reads as follows: I am to remain indoors after dark

every night and am not allowed to leave the bound-
ries of Cooper's Neck Estates without permission
during the day, except to go to school. I should be
eligible for parole in about six months."

"Did they say anything about me?" I asked.

"Touchy subject," Howie replied. "Let's say
that they didn't *encourage* me to seek your company in the future. My mother hasn't forgotten that
you told me to smoke pot, and she dropped a few
hints. She thinks you're sort of . . . well . . . you
know, wild."

"Yeah, that's me, Wild Man Gilbert."

"I wouldn't worry about it," Howie said. "I still
believe you can pick your friends and you can pick
your nose, but . . ."

"I know, Howie, you can't pick your friend's
nose."

"And to tell you the truth, if I had to do it all
over again, you know what I'd do?"

"What?"

"The same exact thing," he said. "I'm not kidding, either. If I gotta go through all those treatments, I want to enjoy myself too. That was the
first time I've really enjoyed myself in months."

"Yeah, but if it isn't good for you . . ."

"So what do they expect me to do?" Howie
asked. "Live in a test tube for the rest of my life?
You've heard of test-tube babies? Meet the first
test-tube teenager."

"You're right."

"Anyway," Howie said, "listen to this brilliant example of medical logic. This morning the doctor told my parents that if I was well enough to go out partying, I was probably well enough to go back to school."

"The vacation's over, huh?"

"Some vacation," Howie said. "I'd rather go to prison on my next one."

CHAPTER
FOURTEEN

It's funny how stories spread around school. It always seems like the ones that are untrue go around faster than the ones that are true. The story of my disappearing from Chunk's party with Katie got around pretty quickly. By lunchtime Rena must have heard, because for the first time since we broke up I caught her looking at me. I hoped she was jealous.

Later I was walking down the hall when I noticed several people around me turn and stare at something near the wall. Following their eyes, I saw a bald person—Howie fumbling with his books in front of his locker.

"Howie, you made it."

"Yeah." He looked tired.

"Didn't see you at the bus stop this morning."

"My doctor wanted to see me once more before I came to school," he said, piling up a mountain of books on the floor in front of his locker. "My mother drove me."

"So how's it going?"

You could see how it was going by the strain on his face. He looked harried. "I gotta read two plays in English, four chapters in American History, make up two lab experiments, and catch up on a month's worth of French," he said. "Forget about calculus. I'm not even gonna try to catch up with that."

"They don't expect you to catch up overnight, Howie."

"Maybe they don't, but I guess I do. It's bad enough feeling like a freak in those classes without having to be a freak who is two months behind."

"A freak?"

"Being bald," Howie said fretfully. "Everyone sees the bald guy, and by now most of them know I've got leukemia too. If I wasn't bald, at least some people wouldn't know that I was sick, but everything draws attention to me."

"Howie, it's only your first day back, you've got to expect some stares," I said. "But everyone will get used to you."

"Yeah, I just wish they wouldn't stare so much." Howie looked down at the pile of books on the floor. "I guess I'm just tired. All I want to do is go home and go to sleep."

"Why don't you leave some of those books with me," I said. "I'll drop them off at your house after soccer practice."

Howie grinned at me. "You want to carry my books home? Does this mean we're going steady?"

"I'm sorry, Howie, but my mother says I'm not old enough to go steady."

Howie shrugged. "I met your girl friend today."

"Rena?"

"She's in almost all my classes. After about the third one we even had desks next to each other, so she introduced herself."

"What'd she say?" I asked.

"She just said she was glad we finally met and that kind of stuff," Howie said. "And she offered to help me out in any subjects I'm having trouble in. I couldn't tell if she was being serious or just trying to be nice."

"I'm sure she meant it," I said, but I didn't tell him that I was surprised. Wasn't it just a few weeks ago that Rena had been mad at me for being too preoccupied with Howie? I wondered how she'd explain her offer to tutor him.

After soccer practice I dropped the books off at Howie's. Mrs. Jamison met me at the door. "Howie's asleep. He said you'd be stopping by," she said. "Thank you, David." For a second I thought she was just going to turn around and slam the door in my face.

"I'm really sorry about the other night," I said. "I knew Howie wouldn't get drunk. He's smarter than that."

Mrs. Jamison smiled a little. "It's all right, David. We were just very worried."

A nervous moment passed. "I know this isn't really my business," I said, "but I hope you'll let Howie go out once in a while. I mean, I know he really enjoys getting out, and I promise next time I'll have him home on time."

I was trying to make Mrs. Jamison smile again, but she didn't. "That's nice of you, David," she said, looking away from me. "But we have to consider Howie's health first. Should he call you when he wakes up?"

"No, I'll see him in school tomorrow."

"All right, good-bye." The door closed. Was it only Howie's health, I wondered, or was she also worried about Howie running with a pack of high school perverts?

About a week later Howie actually did get permission to go to the local movie house with me. When he got into the car, he was thinner and paler than ever and there were scabs on his lips—some side effect of the medication he was taking. But otherwise he was in the best mood I'd seen him in since Chunk's party. Just getting out of the house always improved his spirits, and he said that with Rena's help every Tuesday and Thursday afternoon he was really making progress toward catching up.

"The school's also sending a home tutor," he said, "but I can use all the help I can get."

I still couldn't get over the idea that Rena was tutoring him.

"She doesn't seem any different from anyone else who's offered to help me," he said when I asked about her.

"There have been others?" I asked, surprised.

"Oh, yeah, I guess two or three kids have offered."

I parked the Datsun at the mall where the movie theater was and looked across the seat at him. "I wasn't sure how the other kids were going to react."

Howie nodded. "Yeah, for a while it looked like you were the only person in the world who would talk to me."

He had so much to say that even after the movie started we kept talking until the people in front of us turned around and asked us to be quiet. Then, while Howie watched the flick, I kept thinking how amazing it all was. Here was a guy who was stricken with a disease that might kill him, but his biggest worry was catching up with his schoolwork. Some days he was so tired and ill he couldn't get up to go to school, but other days he'd walk miles just to watch a friend play a soccer match. Life was crazy.

Howie's cheerfulness and the movie seemed to end at the same moment. I guess he knew we had to go back.

"You know, there are people who have actually elected not to have chemotherapy," he said on the way home. "They try it a couple of times and it's so bad, they say forget it."

"Yeah, Howie, but then what happens?"

"The lights go out. Eternal sleep . . . and no homework."

We pulled into his driveway. From the car we could see into the lit kitchen, where Mrs. Jamison sat with a cup of coffee, waiting for the safe return of her son. But Howie seemed reluctant to get out of the car.

"I hate going back in," he said, his fingers resting on the door handle. "It's not like I ever forget I'm sick, but at least when I go out it seems like it's farther away. In there they treat me like I'm sick, and I act like I'm sick. I swear I even feel sicker. It's like there's nothing else to think about except being sick."

For a few moments we just sat in the car, not talking. All my life, when things had gone wrong, I'd always looked for a way to make them right again. If I said the wrong thing, I apologized, or if I broke something, I tried to fix it, or, if someone else had a problem, I tried to help them. But what could I do for Howie? There was only one thing that could make Howie right again, and that was curing him. But no one knew if that could be done.

Howie's mother saw the car and went to the front door and opened it, waiting for Howie to come in. Howie pulled on the car door handle. "I'll bet you twenty dollars the first thing she says is that she talked to her best friend in Florida tonight and it was eighty-two degrees there today," he said.

"She really wants to go back?" I asked.

Howie sighed. "She didn't want to leave in the first place."

CHAPTER
FIFTEEN

The postseason games were held in the second and third weeks of November. There were three sectional matches during the first week, then two regional playoffs that weekend. If we made it through all that, we'd rest and practice for a week and then go to the championships at Cornell for the last weekend.

Sectionals week was crazy—three matches in four days. All we did was eat, sleep, and play soccer. We won our first two matches on Tuesday and Wednesday. The Tuesday match was at home and Howie came to watch. I didn't see him in school Wednesday or Thursday, and on Friday I was only in school half a day, because the team had to leave at noon to travel to a school on the South Shore. We won, and the bus ride home became a near riot, with guys throwing orange peels and balls of crumpled adhesive tape around and singing victory songs. Chunk, Billy, and I tried to sleep on the equipment bags in the back of the bus. We were tired, and all we could think about was leaving early the next morning for Rockland County and our first regional match.

We got back to school around six o'clock. It was dark, but a bunch of fans were waiting for us in the parking lot and they cheered and honked car horns as we stumbled off the bus, dizzy with fatigue and triumph. It had turned colder and so I put my soccer bag down and pulled out a sweater. Around me everyone was talking about the match and giving congratulations. I put on the sweater, zipped up my bag, and stood up to find Rena facing me.

"Howie missed school again today," she said.

I stared at her in the dark, first feeling surprise, then happiness, then confusion. I was surprised to find her there, happy that she was talking to me, but confused that this was the first thing she'd chosen to say. "Do you think he's in the hospital?" I asked.

"Yes, but I was afraid I'd disturb him if I called."

I wasn't sure what to say next. I was grubby and smelly and had to go home and shower, eat, wash my soccer clothes, and go to sleep. Otherwise I would have asked her out for dinner. I looked around and saw Chunk waiting to give me a ride home. "Can I call you later?" I asked.

Rena glanced away. "I, uh, won't be home until late," she said.

"Oh, well." I made a big deal of pointing out Chunk. "I've got to catch a ride home."

Rena nodded and turned away.

"You made up?" Chunk yelled. We were flying down the road from school in his MGB.

"I wish I knew," I said.

At home I threw my soccer stuff into the washing machine, showered, and called Howie's. Mr. Jamison answered.

"Oh, uh, hi, Mr. Jamison. I'm calling about Howie."

"He's back in the hospital, David." Mr. Jamison sounded really low.

"Is he okay?"

"We think so, for the time being at least."

The time being? I wanted to ask what that meant but I didn't. "Can I go see him?" I asked.

"It would be better if you went tomorrow."

We won our match in Rockland, earning us the right to return the next day for the game to determine the regional champions, the last step before the state championship. We played at eleven in the morning and were back in Cooper's Neck by four-thirty. I declined a victory meal with the team and caught a ride home instead.

I got home to discover both my parents were out and there was no car for me to take to the hospital.

The only form of transportation left was my ten-speed, which I hadn't used in so long that the tires had gone flat. I had to blow them up with the hand pump. The sun was just starting to go down as I threw on an extra sweater and pushed off into the cold November afternoon.

I had never measured it, but West Hill must have been about eight miles from our house. Turning onto the main road, I realized I'd forgotten to take gloves, and racing through the cold air, my hands quickly turned red and began to hurt. I soon knew what a dumb mistake I'd made and had to slow up so I could warm one hand in my jacket pocket while I held the handlebars with the other.

Meanwhile, the questions started popping into my head. Was Howie out of remission? Why else would he suddenly return to the hospital? I tried to think of other possible reasons—maybe he had a new infection, or some other complication. But Mr. Jamison's words kept coming back to me—"... *for the time being.*" Howie *was* out of remission. Other thoughts came: "*AML. Hardly anyone recovers.*" I rode faster, both hands back on the handlebars, hunched over like a racer, flying down the shoulder of the road as the sun dropped and it began to grow dark. What was going to happen to Howie after "... *for the time being*"? I had to know. Someone at the hospital would know. A nurse, a doctor, someone.

It was dark when I got to West Hill. My hands

were so stiff and cold, I couldn't unbutton my jacket as I rode up in the elevator. As we stopped on the fourth floor and the doors opened, I felt a chill run up my arms and across my shoulders to my ears. I hesitated a moment and then had to jump out quickly to beat the closing doors. Suddenly I realized how worried I was.

"The soccer player," Howie said when I walked into the room. He looked like a stranger—bald, gaunt, more scabs on his lips, both eyes black and blue as if he'd been in a bad fight. From a bag above him someone else's blood snaked down a plastic tube and through a needle into his arm. Seeing him so pale and sickly I almost asked out loud, *"How could this happen?"*

Instead, I said hello to Mrs. Jamison, who was sitting in a chair across from the bed.

"Hello, David." She was stiff and formal, hiding her feelings as usual.

I tried to act nonchalant. "So what's up, Howie?"

"Transfusion time," he said. "When I went in two days ago for a checkup, they said they'd never seen a blood count so low. I've been on transfusions ever since."

"Are they giving you treatments?" I asked.

"Yeah, but they have to stop and give me some blood once in a while."

With that I had my answer. He must have been out of remission. Did he know it? He had to.

Mrs. Jamison started to put her coat on, saying that now that I was there she'd go home and make dinner for her husband. After she'd gone Howie said he had to admit he was kind of glad. "She's been here all day," he said, shaking his head.

"She's still pissed at me," I said.

"You and everyone," Howie said. "Probably even me for getting so sick." There was a dejected tone in his voice.

"How are things at home?" I asked.

Howie fidgeted with the plastic identification tag around his wrist. "It beats the hospital," he said, "but not by much. Mom complains all the time. The neighbors are unfriendly. It's too cold. It's too expensive. It's too this, and it's too that. It's a drag listening to her."

I figured it was time to change the subject. "Rena told me you weren't in school Friday. She was worried."

"She's really nice," Howie said. "I was hoping that with her and the school tutor I'd be able to catch up by Christmas, maybe even start applying to college for next . . ." Howie blinked and I saw that he was going to cry. I got up and went over to the bed. He was trying to fight the tears. "I've been waiting the whole damn day . . . just to be alone so I could let it out." He was wiping his eyes with his hands, so I pulled some tissues out of a box near the bed and gave them to him.

My hand was on his shoulder and I felt him tremble. "I'm sorry." Howie sniffed. "I just can't hold it in anymore."

"It's okay, pal," I said. Sometimes on the soccer field you'd see a guy get kicked or tripped and a few tears would squeeze out of his eyes, even though he was fighting it. I knew those were the kind of tears Howie was crying.

"It's *so* stupid," Howie insisted. He grabbed some more tissues and blew his nose. "Like in here"—he pointed to his bald head—"I don't think I should be crying, but I can't help it."

"Yeah, don't worry, I won't tell," I said, squeezing his shoulder. We stayed like that for a while, Howie crying quietly and me standing there, not sure what to say and kind of afraid I might start crying any second myself.

"I guess," Howie said after a few moments. "I guess I'm just really scared."

How could you *not* be, I thought. I felt the thinness of his shoulder beneath my hand. It was so eerie that I was touching, holding the shoulder of a living person, someone my own age, who might die. It seemed impossible.

After a while Howie stopped. "I'm sorry, David, this is such a crappy situation," he said, wiping away the last of the tears.

Then we sat for a while without speaking. I'd become used to these long silences with Howie. They'd bothered me at first, but now I realized he just wanted someone to be there. I didn't have to keep him entertained with scintillating conversation for hours on end.

"Do you ever think about dying, David?" Howie asked unexpectedly.

"I have . . ."

"What do you think happens?" he asked.

"I don't think you should talk about it, Howie," I said, frightened by his asking. "I don't think you're in danger of dying." Liar, I told myself.

"I want to know," Howie insisted. "What do you think happens?"

"Well, I think you just turn off. I don't think you go anywhere, and I don't think you . . . are conscious of any pain or of dying."

Howie thought about it for a moment. "I wish I *was* religious," he said. "I wish I was like my grandparents and really believed you went someplace nice like heaven." Then he looked up at me. "Maybe you do, David. Maybe they've been right all along."

I looked away, not knowing how to respond. I didn't believe that and I didn't think Howie really believed it.

"You know, it's the same old thing that keeps coming back to me again and again," Howie said. "I keep asking myself, Why me? What did I do?"

"You didn't do anything, Howie. You know that."

"Maybe I didn't eat right as a kid," Howie went

on, ignoring me. "Maybe I once breathed some fumes or drank some contaminated water . . ."

"Come on, Howie, you know that's—"

"It could even be genetic," Howie insisted, cutting me off. "Some genetic weakness that makes me more susceptible."

"You know that's not true," I said. I could see him getting worked up. "Come on, Howie."

But Howie kept ignoring me. "Maybe it's something science hasn't even figured out yet."

"Howie—"

"Maybe it's—" Howie suddenly grabbed a glass of water from the night table and threw it blindly. It crashed against the wall opposite the bed. He glared at me, tears rushing again from his eyes. "Damn you, David. What the hell do you know," he yelled and then turned away, sobbing.

I was still standing there in shock when a nurse rushed in. "Did something break?" she asked, and at the same moment she saw the crescent of water on the wall and the pieces of broken glass that had fallen on the chair nearby and on the floor.

Howie wiped his reddened eyes with his hand. "It fell," he said.

The nurse was not amused. "I'll get an orderly," she said. "Meanwhile, don't walk around here in bare feet."

"What does she expect me to do?" Howie asked after she left. "An Indian glass dance or something?"

I forced a smile on my face, but I was still shaking from his outburst. An orderly, a young guy, came in and looked at the wall. "Target practice, huh?"

"There was a fly on the wall," Howie said.

The orderly started sweeping the wet glass into a dustpan. "You get 'im?" he asked.

"Sure," Howie said, looking over at me. "You think I'd just go and waste all that water?"

The orderly chuckled and finished his job. Howie and I both watched him silently, avoiding each other's eyes. But when the orderly had left, Howie turned to me. "David," he said, "I'm sorry I said that. You know I didn't mean it."

That night I called Rena's and left a message with her mother for Rena to call me, no matter how late she got in. It was after 2:00 A.M. when she called and my father had to come and wake me up in the den, where I'd fallen asleep in front of the television. I opened my eyes to find him standing over me in his pajamas.

"Do you know what time it is?" he asked angrily, but I was already heading toward the kitchen to get the phone.

"Rena?"

"David, your father got so mad." She was giggling.

I yawned. "I'll wash the cars next week. That'll make him happy."

"You hope," she said.

"I saw Howie tonight in the hospital," I said. "It was really bad. He wanted to know if I ever thought about dying."

On the other end of the line Rena was quiet for a moment. "It's scary, David."

"Yeah." I rubbed my eyes, still trying to wake up. There was a silence on the phone again. Rena was waiting for me to explain why I wanted her to call. "Look, Rena, I know this is going to sound kind of strange, but the reason I wanted you to call was so I could ask you something that really puzzles me. A couple of weeks ago you were pissed off at me because of Howie. But now you're tutoring him and looking for him at school and worrying about him. I don't get it."

Another pause. "And now, at two-thirty in the morning, you want me to explain?" she asked.

"I'll accept an abbreviated version." Pretty witty for 2:30 A.M., I thought.

"Why should I?" Rena asked.

"For old times' sake," I said. "Remember, not too long ago we were lovers."

Rena laughed. "Spare me the melodrama, David."

"You're wasting precious seconds," I said.

"Oh, okay." Rena sighed. "First of all, I was mad at you because I resented the pressure you were putting on me to join your Howie Jamison bandwagon. Second, I was, and am, mad at you for giving up your soccer career. Third, you have become the most overbearing goody-two-shoes imaginable, especially where Howie is concerned. Fourth, I am still skeptical of your decision to go to medical school, David, it sounds maudlin."

"What does that mean?"

"Overly sentimental. You should know that from the SAT's," Rena said. "Anyway, after we broke up—"

"You mean," I said, "after you broke up with me."

Rena cleared her throat. "After that, Howie came to school and he was in some of my classes. I thought he was very nice, and when he asked me if I would help him in some subjects—"

"*He* asked *you?*"

"Well, it was obvious that he needed some help. He was nearly two months behind and anyway, I think he was in a little over his head, especially in French. And since I didn't have *you* badgering me about going to soccer games anymore, I thought I'd—uh—offer."

"Sounds pretty goody-two-shoes maudlin to me," I said.

"I'm going to hang up, David."

"Before you do, Rena, I want you to know that despite all my faults, I'd still like to get back together with you."

"You really think you're cute, don't you?" Rena laughed again and hung up.

CHAPTER
SIXTEEN

I didn't get back to the hospital until Monday. The day before, we won again 2–1 in overtime. The farther we went, the tougher the teams got and the more each match took out of us, both in physical and nervous energy. After staying up to talk to Rena on Saturday night and then playing the match on Sunday, I came home exhausted, spent a few hours trying to catch up on my homework, and fell asleep around nine o'clock.

Howie was alone when I went to see him Monday afternoon. He was wearing the hypothermia blanket again, and the green mat filled with circulating liquid seemed to rest heavily on his chest. He looked tired and pale and sweat dripped off his forehead, as if someone had just squeezed a sponge on him. He hardly smiled at me.

"You got a temperature?" I asked.

"Started getting the sweats last night," he said, sounding cranky. "They keep coming and going." On his lap was a thick book with a technical title about leukemia—some kind of medical text. I waited for Howie to say something more, but he was preoccupied with the book and only occasionally glanced at me. I had never seen him in such a bad mood.

"Where's your mom?"

"I don't know."

The only sound in the room was a faint humming noise the hypothermia machine made as it pumped the water into the mat on Howie's chest. Since Howie didn't want to talk, I just sat there watching him and thinking. During my life I'd had broken bones that had knitted themselves, suffered cuts that had closed, caught colds that had gone away, had sore throats, even the mumps—all ills my body had been strong enough to fight off. But what Howie had frightened me. It wasn't like bacteria or viruses that invade the body from the outside—cancer was something from within, something so bad that Howie's body was incapable of fighting it off by itself. Even the machines and medicines and doctors might not be enough to stop it. And Howie lay there knowing this while we stood around him, watching helplessly.

"Don't look at me like that," Howie said angrily, abruptly bringing my thoughts back to the room. "That's the way my father looks at me. I hate it."

"I'm sorry, Howie," I stammered. "I was just—uh—thinking."

Howie suddenly reached for a pile of books and papers on the night table. "Give these to my French teacher," he said, shoving several sheets of notebook paper at me. "I have to know if I'm doing this stuff right before I go any further."

"Sure." I folded the pages and put them in my jacket. Just then the door opened and a bunch of doctors wearing white jackets and carrying clipboards walked in. It took a second before I realized they weren't all real doctors. One who looked older probably was, but the others looked too young. I figured they were medical students and tried to picture myself among them someday.

"Hello, Howie," said the doctor who was apparently leading the group. He was a tall man with curly gray hair and wire-rimmed glasses. "How are you feeling?"

Howie stared at the group. "Wet," he said, wiping sweat off his forehead.

The tall doctor turned to me and said, "Would you wait outside for a few moments?"

I looked at Howie, but he was no longer aware of me. He was watching the doctor, a tense, worried look on his face.

Out in the hall the few moments stretched into fifteen and then twenty minutes. I leaned against the tile wall and waited. Finally the group of white

jackets came out of Howie's room. They passed
me and started walking down the hall. Instead of
going back into Howie's room, I followed a few
feet behind, getting up the nerve to say, "Excuse
me."

Five white jackets stopped and turned. They
looked surprised.

"I'm a friend of Howie's," I said, nervously
addressing the tall doctor who was in charge. "I've
known him since he got sick and I—well—I was
wondering if I could ask you a question, because I
can't ask anyone else."

"What is it?" the doctor asked.

"Well, I just want to know if Howie's going to
be all right," I said.

The young medical students quickly turned to
the older doctor to see how he dealt with questions
from worried friends of sick patients. The doctor
smiled at me. It seemed important for him to show
the group and me that he was confident and sure
of himself. "We all hope so," he said.

I expected him to say more, but instead he gave
me a big smile and turned with his little entourage
and continued down the hall. I felt like a bother-
some fly who'd just been brushed away, and it
made me mad. I wanted to run down the hall, stop
the doctor, and tell him he hadn't given me a
satisfactory answer. But I didn't.

When I went back into the room, Howie had the

medical text open again on his lap and was reading it.

"That took a while," I said.

Howie glanced at me briefly, and then stared back into the book. For the first time since I'd started visiting him in the hospital, he gave me the feeling he didn't care that I was there, or maybe even wished I wasn't.

"Howie?" I said.

He looked up at me and seemed annoyed that I was disturbing him. "I had a lot of questions. I've been reading up."

"What'd they say?" I asked.

Howie started turning the pages rapidly, as if he was searching for something. "They said it was okay for me to read, but I shouldn't try to diagnose myself or measure my progress by what I read, because every case is different." He paused to look at one of the pages. "I'm beginning to think those doctors are really full of it sometimes."

"How come?"

"They try to make it seem like it's all a big mystery that no one but doctors can understand," he said. He nodded to the book. "But I can read."

"Does the book say something different?" I asked.

Howie shrugged his shoulders. "I can't tell. I have to read some more."

I watched him leaf through some more pages. "Were some of them medical students?"

"Psychiatric interns," Howie said, still turning pages.

"Psychiatric?"

"Yeah, there's a whole psychology about dealing with patients," Howie said. "Especially cancer patients."

"How come?"

Howie wiped some more sweat off his brow and slammed the book closed in frustration. "Because it's such a crappy disease."

CHAPTER SEVENTEEN

Two days later something went wrong with Howie.
I hadn't talked to him since my last visit, but Rena
had gone to the hospital and learned that Howie
was badly in need of blood. Somehow, overnight
she single-handedly organized a blood drive, and
the next morning when I got to school there were
notices up on every bulletin board, explaining
where and when to give blood for Howie. There
was even a carpool to the hospital after classes.
For more information you had to see Sara Parker.
I couldn't believe it, Howie Jamison had become a
cause célèbre.

At lunch Rena asked if I'd join her. After coming out of the food line a few minutes later, I
found her sitting with Sara. Between their lunch
trays was a piece of paper with times and people's
names written on it. It must have been the carpool
schedule.

"Are you getting many volunteers?" I asked, sitting down opposite them.

Rena and Sara looked at each other and then back at me. "Not many," Rena said, sounding downcast.

"Can you go?" Sara asked.

"I don't know. I've got the state championship this weekend. I better find out what kind of effect giving blood would have."

Sara looked shocked. "Isn't Howie more important than soccer?"

I had to chuckle. "Sara, a month ago you didn't even want us to talk about Howie at your dinner party. Back then the most important thing was your grouse."

Sara's eyes went wide, but before she could retaliate, Rena intervened. "Hold it!" She turned to Sara, and then to me. "I'll call the hospital and ask," she said. "I don't think anyone on the soccer team should give blood if it will hurt their chances next weekend."

Sara looked at her in disbelief. "Are you serious?"

But Rena only said, "I'll explain it to you later."

"If it's okay, I might be able to get some guys from the team," I said. "I can't promise anything, but I'll try."

After lunch Rena and I went down to the guidance office. Because she was organizing the blood campaign for Howie, Rena was allowed to use the office phone. It was obvious that the administration thought it was simply marvelous that Rena was performing such a noble service, and I had to admit I was a little jealous. After all, I'd been the first to befriend Howie, why should Rena get all the glory?

She called West Hill and spoke to someone in the blood donor room.

"You shouldn't give whole blood," she said later as we walked back to the cafeteria. "But you can give platelets today or tomorrow and be all right for the game on Saturday."

"I'll see if I can get any guys," I said.

We were approaching the entrance to the cafeteria, but Rena stopped and stood in the hall. "I wish you'd be nicer to Sara, David," she said.

"Why should I?" I asked.

"It could help things," she said. A coy smile appeared out of nowhere.

"Things?"

"Between you and me."

I must have stood there looking like a dodo for a while. Then Rena smiled and quickly walked into the cafeteria, leaving me standing there alone. Typical Rena style, just like Hiroshima: drop the big one and get out fast. Did it mean she wanted us to get back together? Well, if she did, why didn't she just say so? Did she really think she could keep playing games with me? Ha!

I went down to the athletic offices before practice to ask Coach Lavelle if he would talk to the team about giving blood. Lavelle was on the phone, but he waved me in. "That's right," he was saying. "Seven rooms, each with two beds. No, it doesn't matter if they're double beds or single."

I sat down in a chair opposite his desk and looked around the room. It was lined with dusty trophies and old photos of championship teams, mostly tennis and cross-country and one really old football picture. There were no pictures of soccer teams.

Lavelle got off the phone. "Well, I just made reservations for Cornell. I wish someone would tell me why I'm more excited about this championship than my team."

"We're just too cool," I said.

"As always," Lavelle said. "So what can I do for you, David?"

I told him about Howie and about how he needed blood and wasn't getting a great turnout from the kids at school. "I was hoping maybe you'd talk to the team," I said. "We called the hospital, and if we give platelets today or tomorrow, we'll be okay for the game on Saturday."

Coach Lavelle leaned back in his chair, his hands folded on his lap. It was obvious that he wasn't crazy about the idea. "I don't know, David. If I speak to the team, some of the boys may feel pressured because I'm their coach. I think they should feel that whether or not they give blood has nothing to do with their standing on the team. You understand?"

I nodded.

"And you're sure it won't affect you for the championship?"

"We talked to a nurse in the donor room," I said.

"Okay," Lavelle said. "You talk to the team before practice. But let me give you a word of advice. Don't try to force or embarrass anyone into giving blood. Just state your case the way you did to me and see who volunteers. I know you think this is very important, but you have to understand that not everyone sees it like you."

"I can't believe anyone would think a kid's life wasn't important," I said.

Coach Lavelle rubbed his hands laboriously against his forehead. "You wouldn't think so, would you."

Later I tried writing some notes, but everything I wrote down sounded like it was straight out of a Jerry Lewis telethon. I had no idea what I was going to say, even as Lavelle was telling the team to get together in the middle of the locker room. Some of the guys had been my teammates for five or six years—guys I'd taken hundreds of showers with—but standing up in front of them I felt so nervous I clasped my hands behind my back so they couldn't see them trembling.

"Listen," I said. "I don't want to take time from practice, but there's this guy in West Hill. His name's Howie and some of you have met him already and you know he's sick. Anyway, something went wrong yesterday and he needs blood transfusions. Anyone can give blood today or tomorrow and still be in good shape for the game Saturday. So if you want to, you can go with me to the hospital tomorrow after practice."

A crowd of blank faces stared up at me. I knew the speech hadn't been long enough. It hadn't sounded important enough. "I know it's a lot to ask," I said, trying to think of something more to say. "And I wouldn't be up here if he didn't really need it."

It still wasn't enough. How could you explain it in just a few words? I didn't know. No one said a thing. Not that I expected everyone to jump up and volunteer at once, but the silence was so heavy that I was sure I'd be going alone to the hospital the next day. Hardly anyone would even look at me. Then Billy Lee raised his hand. "I'll go tomorrow."

"You can't," Johnny Jarret said. "You're the wrong race."

A couple of guys cracked up. "I don't think it makes a difference," I said.

Several guys nodded, but no new hands went up. Lavelle stood up. "Okay, boys, let's go," he said, pushing open the door that led out to the field. "And give it some thought. The boy needs your help."

Outside I caught up to Chunk, who was jogging out to the field alone. "You think a couple of pints of blood are gonna make a difference?" he asked sourly.

"I don't know, Chunk."

"Well, I wouldn't get your hopes up," he said. "Once they start needing a lot of blood, it's usually the beginning of the end."

I stopped running. After all the frustrations that day, I didn't need to hear crap like that. Chunk ran a few feet more and then he stopped too. Most of the team was already ahead of us, but a few guys passed, giving us funny looks.

"You know, you can be a real jerk sometimes, Chunk." I was really pissed.

"Yeah, why's that?" he asked.

"Because you just don't say things like that. Whether they're true or not. Nobody wants to hear it, especially me."

Chunk stepped back toward me. "Well, you better learn to listen, because it's not a big fairy tale, David. You don't just pour the blood in and expect them to be fine."

"And how do you know?" I asked.

"Because I saw it happen with my aunt. The whole damn family was in there giving blood, and what difference did it make?"

"So you won't give now?"

Chunk shrugged. "The hell with it."

"You know, Chunk, if people like you would stop being such lousy pessimists all the time, someone like Howie might have a chance," I said. "And I'll tell you something else. I am sincerely sorry your aunt died, but I think you're just using her as an excuse for copping out. I think being pessimistic is just a cover-up. The easiest way to get out of doing anything for anyone is to say it's all hopeless anyway. Why don't you just tell the truth, Chunk? You don't feel like helping, do you?"

I guess we were arguing pretty loudly because most of the team was watching us now. Chunk took another step toward me, his face growing red. "Since we're getting everything off our chests, Mr. Righteous, I think it's about time someone told you that you're getting to be a real pain with your save Howie crusade. Ever since you got to know him, you've been pulling this holier-than-thou crap all over the place, like you're some kind of saint or something." Then he put his hands together like he was praying and said in a high, squeaky voice, " 'Oh, Chunk, please give poor Howie a ride home' and 'Oh, Chunk, please invite poor Howie to your party' and 'Please give some blood for poor Howie.' Just because he's sick doesn't give you the right to—to act like such a flake."

I don't know who made the first move, but a

second later we were trying to wrestle and punch each other to the ground. I must have been out of my mind, because Chunk was twice as strong as me. I don't think I even managed to hit him, but he punched me hard on the cheekbone under my left eye. Moments later a dozen arms were pulling us apart.

No one even bothered to ask what the fight was about. I guess they could hear. Lavelle ordered everyone into line for calisthenics. Chunk and I made sure we were as far apart as we could be.

All during practice I wondered if he was right about me acting like a saint. Rena had said things like that on the phone too. Maybe I had come on too strong about Howie, but I was certain that it was the right thing to do. Maybe it wouldn't make me the most popular guy on the block, but damn it, some things were more important than being Mr. Cool Popular Nice Guy who never bothered anyone about anything. Sure, everyone wanted to be cool, so cool that a nuclear bomb going off in their faces wouldn't ruffle any feathers. But did that mean you were supposed to be cool while someone you knew needed your help to stay alive? It was easy to say, "Let someone else give blood," but if everyone was as cool as that then forget it. Howie wouldn't stand a chance.

Still, in a way I was glad Rena was running the blood drive and not me.

After practice Chunk and I sat next to each other at our lockers, pulling off our dirty soccer clothes, practically rubbing shoulders, but not talking or even looking at each other. I knew that he knew that it was pretty silly for both of us to sit there and not talk, but I was damned if I was going to be the one who started talking first. Besides, my cheek throbbed painfully. Even if it had been a real fight, Chunk didn't have to hit me *that* hard.

"Hey, Count Dracula, you want blood?" Johnny Jarret was standing at the end of the bench, naked except for a towel around his waist.

"Shut up, Jarret." I was in no mood for his jokes.

Johnny frowned. "Don't be a nerdball, man. I was only coming over to ask what time you're going tomorrow."

I smiled. Chunk was unwrapping the tape from his feet. He had to be listening. "We'll do half a practice and then go," I said.

"Okay, just don't forget me," Johnny said. With that he went down to the showers. Wonder of wonders.

I was still up doing my homework around 11:30 that night when the phone rang. My heart pole-vaulted about ten feet on the chance that it was Rena. I'd been thinking about her all evening, but I'd resisted the temptation to call her, since I was sure that was what she wanted me to do.

"Hello?"

"Look, uh, I'll go with you tomorrow on one condition, okay?" It was Chunk.

"What's that?"

"That you stop acting like a sister of mercy," he said.

"Deal, Chunk, but you know, my face feels like it met a Mack truck in a dark alley."

"Sorry, partner."

CHAPTER
EIGHTEEN

Of the six of us who went to West Hill the next afternoon, only Chunk had given blood before. No one wanted to admit he was nervous, but in one way or other everyone showed it. We were all in Billy's Le Mans—three in the front seat and three, including two sophomores Rena had asked us to take, in the back. Billy was absolutely silent the entire way, Chunk was gloomy, the two sophomores squirmed nervously, and Johnny talked nonstop.

"Will you shut up already," Chunk yelled irritably at Johnny.

"Aw, suck on a root, Lowell."

Every time Johnny said something filthy, the sophomores giggled.

Chunk glared at them. "Look, what's with you two? You gay or something?"

The sophomores giggled even harder.

Now Johnny got on them. "You better not be gay," he said. "You see what Lowell did to Gilbert's eye?"

Yes, they'd seen. Overnight my left eye had developed a gorgeous shiner. By breakfast I looked like half of the Lone Ranger.

"This guy," Johnny said, pointing at Chunk, "is certified as dangerous and prone to acts of irrational violence. And he *hates giggling*."

By the time we got to the hospital the two sophomores were so hyped up they practically leaped out of the car.

There were signs everywhere directing us to the donor room and in no time we crowded into an elevator and rode down to the basement level. "Maybe it'll get stuck," Johnny prayed while we were inside. But no such luck, the doors opened and directly across the hall was a big sign with DONOR ROOM printed on it, in red.

Johnny stopped and pretended he was reading an invisible plaque above the doorway. "Abandon all hope ye who enter . . ." We shoved him through the doors.

A nurse, who looked about my mother's age, was sitting at a desk inside. "Can I help you?" she asked.

Six of us crowded around the little desk. "We want to give platelets for Howie Jamison."

"All of you?" the nurse seemed flustered.

"Unless you can just drain everything out of

these two kids," Johnny said, pointing at the sophomores, "and skip us."

"Well, we can't take you all at once, we only
have four beds available."

"Aw, shucks." Johnny turned to leave but Chunk
grabbed him.

"But some beds will be available later if you
want to wait," the nurse said.

We said we would.

She called over another nurse and the two of
them took down our medical information on forms.
Next it was time to get our fingers pricked. Johnny
was talking a mile a minute now. "Listen," he
told us, just before the nurse pricked his finger.
"If I don't make it, win the championship for me."

The nurse sighed and jabbed him.

"The process is called plasmaphoresis," we were
told. "We remove your blood, separate the platelets in a centrifuge, and return the rest to you. It
takes about two hours."

"Two hours! What do you take, a couple of
gallons?"

"Shut up, Jarret."

"Who wants to go first?" the nurse asked.

We decided the two sophomores and Johnny
and Billy would go, and Chunk and I would visit
Howie. "Bury me on the soccer field," Jarret yelled
out as we left.

Chunk and I had to walk through some under-
ground corridors to get to the Solomon Cohen

Pavilion. The halls were cold and empty and we walked without talking. I knew something was still bothering Chunk.

"What is it, Chunk?" I said. "Am I still acting like too much of a saint?"

Chunk shook his head. "You could've told me you were quitting soccer," he said.

He must have found out I wasn't taking a scholarship. I grabbed his arm and stopped. I could tell it really bothered him, maybe even hurt him. "I'm not quitting, Chunk. I just don't think I want to be a pro. I don't even know if I could be one if I wanted to."

Chunk nodded slowly and stuck his hands in his back pockets. "You're gonna be a doctor?" he asked skeptically.

"I'm gonna try."

"How come?"

How did you answer that? It was a gut feeling: soccer—no, doctor—yes. I couldn't explain it. How does anyone know what they want to do—other than just feeling that it's right for them? If I lived my life and looked back at the end and saw that I'd been a soccer player, I'd feel it wasn't worthwhile. But I couldn't tell that to Chunk. Maybe he'd look back and see that it was worthwhile.

"Chunk, what if I got out of college and found that no teams wanted me? What are there, about six hundred professional soccer jobs in the United States? What would I do if I wasn't good enough?"

"You could always play indoor soccer," he said.

I waved the idea away. "That's not soccer, it's human pinball."

Chunk looked down the hall. I knew what he was thinking. We'd never talked about as many personal things as we had in those last few weeks, and it still made us uncomfortable. Things we never dreamed would happen. Like Howie getting so sick and me quitting soccer. Those old days, when everyone stayed healthy and we were all going to become professional soccer players, were over.

"I'm not saying you and Billy shouldn't do it, Chunk," I said, trying to make him feel better. "I'm just saying it isn't for me."

Chunk nodded, but I could see he either didn't understand or didn't believe me. Without speaking, we started down the corridor to Howie's room again.

As sick as he was from the chemotherapy treatments and the disease, Howie seemed glad to see us. But this was the worst I'd ever seen him—he looked like a little old bald man, thinner than ever, and his skin was an awful grayish color. He lay in the bed as if he was unable to pull himself out of it. Even his voice had lost its strength. "How'd you get that?" he asked, staring at my black eye.

I nodded at Chunk. "He gave it to me."

Howie scowled. He must have thought I was kidding him, but he let it pass.

"Rena organized a blood drive at school," I told him.

"Yeah." Howie smiled slightly. "They got it under control now. But I still need platelets." Just speaking seemed to tire him and he had to pause between sentences.

"The team's doing really well," I said, not waiting for Howie to ask. "We're going to the championships this weekend." I continued talking about the team. Howie would listen and then he would fade out for a little while and come back. Chunk was quiet, but the expression on his face said plenty. This was the first time he'd visited Howie in the hospital and he kept staring at the tubes running into Howie's arms and the battlefield of black, blue, and red marks inside his forearms. Under the bed sheets we could see the outline of Howie's thin body. It almost seemed as if he'd shrunk.

The nurse in the donor room had given us an extension number and told us to call, in case a bed became free. On our first try we learned one had been vacated. Chunk said he'd go down. Howie smiled when we told him a bunch of soccer players were downstairs giving platelets. As Chunk got up to leave, Howie thanked him.

"No sweat," Chunk said. He closed the door.

"Where's your mom?" I asked Howie when Chunk was gone.

Howie looked down and smoothed the sheets with his hands. "I asked her not to come today," he said.

"How come?"

"She's been getting on my nerves," he said. "I don't like being here alone all day, but at least it's peaceful." I waited for him to say something more, but he looked out the window. It was a cold, gray day. Most of the trees had lost their leaves and the ones that hadn't were a dull brown. It occurred to me that almost three months had passed since Howie first got sick.

"She wants to go back," Howie said.

"Seriously?" I asked.

Howie nodded slightly. "She got my dad to ask for his old job back. She really hates it up here."

"Why?" I asked, even though I had a feeling I knew.

"I don't know. She blames everything that's happened . . . on the North. I get sick and it's the North's fault. If it's hard to make new friends, it's the North's fault. Even if the car gets a flat tire, it's the North's fault." He paused and smiled. It was supposed to be a joke. Then he reached for a cup of water on the night table. I watched as he dipped his tongue into the cup and then touched it to his cracked, scabbed lips, gently dampening them.

"You want to go back?" I asked.

"Sometimes," he said. "I think that if we go back to Florida—after I get better—it would be like nothing ever happened. Like we never moved north and I never got sick. We could be right back where we started. The only difference would be the time that passed."

"But you've made friends here."

"Yeah," Howie said, "I know."

Then the phone rang. It was Johnny Jarret, informing me that there was a bed available in the donor room.

Giving blood wasn't so bad, except that after they took it you had to sit around for forty-five minutes while they put it through the centrifuge and separated the platelets from the red blood cells. As the nurse explained, we could do without the platelets for Saturday's game, but we had to get our red blood cells and plasma back. Johnny, Billy, and the sophomores were just getting their blood back when I went down to give mine. Chunk had already given and was waiting while it went through the centrifuge. Everyone was pretty quiet when I got down there. No one even asked me how Howie was. Chunk must have told them.

When they were finished, one of the sophomores called his mother, who came and took his friend and Johnny home. Billy and Chunk waited, sitting on the donor bed next to the one where I lay. They both looked pretty depressed.

"Hey, Chunk," I said, "anyone ever tell you that giving blood makes you turn kind of orange?"

"It's that Tan-o-rama place," he said, slowly knocking the heels of his cowboy boots together. "I'm gonna have to stop going there, before I turn the color of Sara Parker's Corvette."

"What're you gonna do?"

"Take an extra week off around Christmas and go to Saint Martin with my cousin," he said. "That should tide me over till Easter vacation."

Billy nudged him with his elbow. "Every day you sound more like a cowboy," he said.

We were still chuckling when the nurse came in with a red bag of blood and hooked it up to the rack over my head. "Hey," I said, pointing to Chunk. "This guy turned orange after you gave him his blood back."

The nurse looked at Chunk and frowned. "That's so unhealthy for your skin."

"Yeah, but it looks great," Chunk said, grinning at her.

Apparently the nurse didn't think it was funny. "Just wait until forty years from now when your skin is all wrinkled and cancerous. You'll see how great it looks then." She left Chunk looking like he'd just been cut from soccer forever.

"Aw, the hell with her, Chunk," I said. "What does she know?"

Chunk shrugged. Even Billy looked bummed out. "All this talk about cancer," he said. "It makes you feel like sooner or later everyone's gonna get it."

"You know that's not true," I said. But neither Billy nor Chunk appeared to hear me. I guess for the first time in our lives we were understanding that things like disease and death could happen to us. You grow up thinking you're pretty much invulnerable and then one day you meet someone like Howie, someone your own age, and bang—it hits you.

The bag drained into my arm and the nurse removed the needle and gave me a bandage. Without talking we left the hospital and got into Billy's car. Chunk sat in the back and pulled the brim of his cowboy hat down over his eyes. I'd never seen him as sulky as he'd been lately. Billy tore out of the parking lot as if he never wanted to come back to the hospital again.

On the way home I decided I wanted to see Rena. Billy said he'd drop me off at her house.

Billy let me out in the Steubens' driveway. It was dark out and as I walked toward the slate path to the front door I noticed that someone inside the house was turning off the lights. Just as I got to the front door it opened. Rena and her mother, both wearing fur coats, were coming out.

"David!"

"Uh, hi, Rena, hi, Mrs. Steuben."

Mrs. Steuben smiled at me. She always smiled at me in this amused way, as if to say that she understood the tribulations of young love.

"I guess I caught you going out," I said.

"We're going to the city to a show," Rena said. She was wearing some makeup and lipstick and her hair was combed out over the coat and she looked about twenty-five years old and beautiful. "Why didn't you call?"

"We were coming back from the hospital and I asked Billy to drop me off. Sort of on impulse."

"How will you get home?" she asked.

"I don't know. I guess I'll walk. It's not that far."

"No, we'll drop you off," Mrs. Steuben said. "We have time." She walked past us and toward the garage, leaving Rena and me alone.

"Four guys from the team and those two kids gave blood," I said.

"I wish I could get six more donors," Rena said. "I hope we get at least a carload tomorrow. More teachers have said they'd give than students."

In the background we heard the sound of the electric garage door opening. I felt like I had to cram a few hours of conversation into fifteen seconds. There were a lot of things I wanted to say about Howie and the hospital and how I felt, but I couldn't find the words that would say it all so fast. Rena was looking through her bag for a cigarette. She found one and lit it.

"I'm glad you came," she said.

"Yeah, so am I." Brilliant conversation, I thought.

Rena turned her head and blew smoke into the cold air. We heard the car start. "Listen, Rena," I said. "I guess I was pretty overbearing and maudlin, but I've really tried to control it. And you, Chunk, and Sara haven't exactly been uncaring about Howie lately. Now I also happen to know, from an authority on the topic, that I love you. So I think we ought to get back together."

Rena blinked a couple of times. "David," she said softly. "I'm sorry about what happened. I wish I hadn't left you that note."

"I never got a chance to tell you what a good picture it was," I said.

Rena smiled and suddenly I knew I could kiss her. I was just about to put my arms around her when Mrs. Steuben came charging down the driveway in their silver Seville. I opened the passenger door for Rena and then got in the back.

"How is Howie?" Mrs. Steuben asked as we left the driveway.

"I don't know, Mrs. Steuben. I get the feeling he's not doing too well."

"That's such a shame," Mrs. Steuben said.

FRIENDS TILL THE END

Rena looked over the seat at me, smiling sympathetically. I pretended her eyes were saying, "*I love you. Let's go to the same college and live together in an apartment off-campus.*" I smiled back at her, trying to make my eyes say, "*Sure, but we gotta find a cheap place or my old man will have a fit.*"

CHAPTER
NINETEEN

I picked up Rena on the way to the hospital Friday afternoon, the day before we went to Cornell for the championship.

"Did you know that Bobby gave blood for Howie last night?" she asked after she got into the car.

"Tuckel?"

"I saw him showing someone the needle mark this morning," she said. "I think he wants people to think he shot heroin."

"Figures," I said as we turned onto the road to the hospital.

"Come on, David, laugh. It's funny."

"Ha, ha." I was in a lousy mood. Chunk had decided to go to Southern Methodist University in Texas, a school famous for its football team, but almost unknown for soccer. But Chunk said the soccer team was going to be one of the best in the country by the time he graduated. Billy thought Chunk just wanted to be a cowboy.

Something about Chunk had changed and it bothered me. All week he'd been friendly, but at the same time a little distant. I felt like I'd been excommunicated somehow from the little soccer religion we'd been faithful to all through high school. I had the feeling that once we graduated, Chunk would go to Martha's Vineyard for the summer, and then to Southern Methodist, and I'd never hear from him again. It didn't seem fair that just because I didn't want to be a soccer player, I had to lose a friend.

Rena watched the road for a while and then turned and said, "You know, you just went through a red light."

"I did?" I hadn't even seen it. "What's wrong?"

I told her about Chunk going to Texas and my excommunication.

"You're sure you're not imagining it?"

"I don't know, Rena," I said. "The thing Chunk and I always shared was soccer. You know what he said to me after Sara broke up with him?"

"What?"

"That he didn't belong in that crowd anyway. Now he probably thinks that I don't belong to his crowd anymore. I don't even know if he's conscious of it, but it's true."

It was turning dusk as we got to the hospital,

and we walked up the sidewalk to the front entrance, pulling our jackets closed against the cold. Ahead of us I saw a man step through the glass doors, leaving the hospital. It was the doctor I'd stopped in the hall that day a few weeks before. The one who'd brushed me off so easily.

Suddenly I wasn't heading for the hospital entrance anymore.

"David?" Rena called behind me.

"Wait, I'll be right back." I jogged a few steps to catch up to him. "Excuse me, sir." He turned around, just as he had that day in the hospital corridor, except now he was wearing street clothes and we were outside the hospital.

"Yes?"

"My name is David Gilbert," I said. "I'm a friend of Howie Jamison's, and I'm really worried about him."

The doctor blinked and his mouth seemed to grow tight around his lips. "I understand," he said.

"I just want to know how he is," I said. "I mean, it's really hard to see him every day and not know what's happening."

"I'm sorry, David," the doctor said, "but you have to realize that I can't discuss Howie's case with you. It's against the rules of the profession." He looked around as if he was eager to get to his car.

"But don't *you* realize how unfair that is?" I

asked. "Leaving us in the dark when we really care about him. I mean, we don't even know if—"

The doctor looked sharply at me. He knew what I was going to say, but I said it anyway.

"If he's going to live or die."

The doctor frowned. "I'm very sorry, David. I can't help you." He started to walk away.

I moved so quickly it surprised us both. Suddenly I was standing in the doctor's path, blocking the way. He stopped and I could see he wasn't completely sure I wouldn't jump him. Rena had been walking toward us, but in my peripheral vision I saw her stop.

"*It's not fair*," I said again, feeling the words leave my throat with more force than before. "You have to tell me something because I'm going crazy walking in there every day and seeing him and not knowing. Is he getting better?"

The doctor looked away from me and didn't answer.

"Is he?" I demanded.

Now the doctor turned back to me. "You see him every day, David," he said. "What do your eyes tell you?"

"He's not getting better," I said reflexively. "He's getting worse."

The doctor said nothing. He didn't have to. It was as if I'd known it all along. He stepped around me with long, quick strides. Even when I heard

the car engine start I just stood there, looking
down at the asphalt parking lot. He could have
run right into me for all I cared at that moment.
The car rolled past me and toward the exit. As the
noise of the car engine died away I could hear a
softer sound: Rena crying.

CHAPTER
TWENTY

We didn't stay with Howie very long that evening. They'd given him some kind of pain killer that made him groggy and for most of our visit he acted like someone who'd just been awakened from a deep sleep. Once, in the middle of a sentence, his eyes just closed and he stopped talking. It was scary. Then he opened them again and apologized. But he couldn't remember what he'd been talking about and you could see how it frustrated him to be hampered by the drugs. Finally he yawned and said he couldn't stay awake any longer. Rena and I said good-bye. By the time we got to the door, Howie's eyes were already closed.

Rena's mother was staying in the city and we went back to her house that night. We were both really depressed about Howie. Now that we knew, or at least had an inkling of what was to come, we wished we didn't. After all, how could you be encouraging and optimistic when you knew the truth? How could you be cheerful and hopeful when there wasn't any hope? It was worse than unfair—it was cruel. To everyone.

In the kitchen Rena made some scrambled eggs. I sat at the table and watched her. I had never seen her so upset, and in a way I felt bad that she had met Howie and had gotten to like him. Now she was just one more person who had to suffer with him. "Well, I guess there's nothing left for us to do except be his friend," I said. "That's probably all he wants from us anyway."

Across the kitchen Rena lit a cigarette and looked at me through the rising smoke. "I never thought this would happen," she said.

"You mean to Howie?" I asked.

"No," Rena said. "I mean to me."

We talked for a long time that evening. After a while, when there didn't seem to be anything left to say about Howie, we talked about Chunk and Sara. And when we had exhausted them as a topic, we talked about photography and soccer, although they didn't seem so important, not as important as they'd once been. Finally there didn't seem to be anything left to talk about except the subject of us.

I volunteered to make some coffee and got up to put the water on. In a way I wanted to know what Rena was thinking, but in another way I didn't. It was obvious that we were back together, but if it was just over concern for Howie or to give Rena something to do until college, then I wasn't interested. Rena could find someone else to be her jester. In the middle of measuring a scoop of coffee for the drip filter, the words finally came out: "Rena, I don't want us to get back together unless you're really serious, okay? I mean it. Do me a favor and don't string me along."

Rena looked startled. "Really, David, I thought you were going to ask me if I wanted cream and sugar."

"Not funny."

Rena smiled. "Admit it, David, it was."

I shrugged. "Do I get an answer?"

Rena looked around. "Let's go into the living room," she said.

We put our cups and the coffee pot on a tray and left the kitchen. In the living room Rena crushed out her cigarette in the ashtray and poured the coffee. I waited, hoping that she was getting ready to talk.

"When we started dating last year," she said, looking down at her coffee cup, "I wasn't very serious about you."

"I know."

Rena glanced at me for a moment. "I can't completely explain it. I think I was bored and I wanted to get to college and the real world as fast as possible. High school seemed so silly and immature."

"And among the things you found silly and immature were high-school boys asking you out on dates," I added for her. "So you figured you could get a nice, safe boyfriend. Someone to tell the other guys you were taken. Someone you wouldn't have to worry about getting too involved with, so that when it was time to go to college, you could just end it and be on your way."

"It sounds terrible," Rena said.

"I won't argue with that," I said.

"When Howie got sick, you were so different," she said. "At first I didn't like it. It wasn't like you . . . well, actually, it wasn't like the person I wanted you to be, the person I'd always thought you were."

"Just another dumb jock, huh?" I couldn't resist saying it.

Rena reached for my hand and squeezed it. "When I broke up with you, it wasn't really that I didn't want to see you anymore. I just wanted to try to change you back to the David I used to know, the David I didn't have to take seriously. But even that didn't work. You didn't change back, and I missed you. I never thought I'd miss you like that." Rena blushed. "I'm sorry, David."

"But you still haven't answered my question," I said. "Is this serious?"

Rena smiled and kissed me. "Yes, David, this *is* serious."

* * *

186

There's this myth in sports that you shouldn't make love on the night before a big game, but the way I figured it, most of the other guys on my team didn't even have the option. So I didn't think they'd mind. Besides, I knew if I mentioned it to Rena, she'd convince me that it was just a silly superstition.

Sometime later the grandfather clock in the corner of the living room rang twice, and I was vaguely aware that I was supposed to be at home and in bed getting a good night's sleep before the big games coming up over the weekend at Cornell. It was really hard to leave Rena, but I knew it was after two in the morning, and I started to ease myself out of her arms.

"I've got to go home," I whispered.

"No." She held tight.

"I gotta go," I said.

"When will you be back?" she asked.

"Sunday evening before dinner. Why don't you come over and have dinner with us."

Rena said she would, and I got up and started to dress. But as I walked toward the front door I felt a tug on the sleeve of my jacket. "Hey, you," Rena said. I turned around and we kissed again. Even after the kiss, she held on as if she didn't want me to go. After all those months when she didn't seem to care, feeling her care now felt so good I almost didn't leave.

"Rena?" I said as I finally drew away from her. "You'll still be like this when I get back, won't you? I mean, you won't change your mind or anything, right?"

Rena smiled. "Don't worry." She kissed me one last time. "And good luck this weekend."

The door closed behind me and I walked out into the cold night, feeling tired, but great.

CHAPTER
TWENTY-ONE

It was still dark when the alarm went off the next morning. I practically sprang out of bed, instantly nervous and excited. That mixture of feelings didn't leave me particularly inclined toward eating breakfast, but not only had Coach Lavelle instructed us to have a big breakfast, he'd even dictated the menu: "Cereal, toast, eggs, and juice. No bacon, tea, or coffee. Pack a light lunch—sandwich, piece of fruit, some raisins, and drink a lot of liquids."

I was mixing a pitcher of orange juice when my mother, dressed in a robe and rubbing her eyes, came in.

"You didn't have to get up," I said. The way my mother wandered uncertainly into the kitchen, I wasn't sure that she *had* woken up.

She yawned. "I thought I'd cook you breakfast."

That was okay with me.

"You were out late last night," my mother said. "I thought with the trip today you'd be in bed early."

"So did I, but something came up."

"Something that begins with an *r* and ends with an *a* and has long dark hair?" my mother asked.

"You have spies or something?"

My mother smiled. "No, but when my son comes home humming to himself at two in the morning after three weeks of moping around, the choice of explanations narrows."

She had a point.

"Does this mean you're back together?" she asked.

"I guess."

My mother sighed and beat three eggs in a bowl. "Either you constantly pull my leg, or you live in a world with so much insecurity that it would drive any normal person crazy," she said. The eggs hit the skillet and the kitchen filled with sizzling sounds. The toast came up and a few moments later there was a full plate before me. My mother stood at the kitchen counter and poured herself a cup of coffee. "You know, on Monday Mr. Jamison called your father and said they were putting their house back on the market."

The news didn't surprise me, but it did make me sad. "Howie says his mother really wants to move back south."

"It's such a shame," my mother said.

I ate my breakfast in silence. I wondered if it was anyone's fault, but if it was, it was hard to say whose. Mrs. Jamison's for having a chip on her shoulder from the beginning? The residents of Cooper's Neck for not taking time from their shopping and tennis to make friends with her? Maybe it was either everybody's fault or no one's. Or maybe it was just life.

We rode up to Cornell in a chartered bus and the team was crazy with nervous energy. It's only a championship, I kept telling myself, but I was as excited as anyone. It was like being two different people. I cared, but I didn't care. I was excited, but I knew there was nothing really to be excited about. It was just a dumb game, but it was also the culmination of six years of trying to reach the championships. I didn't want to leave Howie for two days, but I didn't want to come back and find him worse, either. I wanted to see him better, by some miracle.

That afternoon we played our first match—the semifinals against one of the three other regional winners—on a soccer field at the upper end of the Cornell campus. We won 3–1. Afterward we showered, had dinner at the motel where we were staying, and spent the evening in our rooms, watching television and talking about the championship game the next day—for most of us the final match of our high school careers. Lavelle hadn't assigned us roommates, we were supposed to find them ourselves. Chunk roomed with Billy. Johnny stayed with me.

The next morning we were directed to the stadium clubhouse and got dressed in a real grown-up locker room, complete with whirlpool machines, a sauna, and unlimited clean towels. Some of the local sports writers had come up for the game and they milled around the dressing room, asking questions and giving encouragement. A couple of them asked me why I hadn't accepted a scholarship, and when I explained that I didn't want one, the writers shook their heads wonderingly. Lavelle watched us, glancing often at his wristwatch until the time came. "Okay, boys," he said, "get out there."

There's nothing stranger than the first time you walk into a stadium filled with cheering people and look up into the stands to see rows of faces looking right back down at you.

"I feel like pulling down my shorts," Johnny mumbled as we jogged onto the field for warm-ups. It was cold, we were well into November, and most of the warm-ups were really just to keep us warm. At the other end of the field our opponents, Western Regional Champions from Utica, were going through their warm-ups. We watched them and they watched us, but there wasn't much you could tell. We'd know soon enough, as soon as the game began.

Even though we were only warming up, I was diving for balls, crashing against the hard, cold earth. Up at Cornell it had to be about ten degrees colder than out on Long Island. The ball felt hard as a rock and every time it hit my hands they stung. But the next ninety minutes were all that mattered now. We could nurse our wounds later.

Just before the game began Coach Lavelle called us to the bench. We were already gassed on chocolate bars and Gatorade. Some players sat, huddled under sweat shirts and warm-up blankets. Others stood, rubbing or blowing into their hands, hopping up and down to keep warm, while Lavelle gave the pep talk.

"Okay, boys," he said, trying to sound like a tough coach. "You got here because you wanted to win. Now, what do you want today?"

"Hot chocolate," one player said.

"A heating pad," said another.

"Ninety-two degrees, clear, and sunny," said a third.

Coach Lavelle sighed and shook his head. "You boys are the biggest bunch of wise-guys I've ever coached."

"Yeah, but we're lovable."

"And we eat our candy bars."

The starting whistle blew and eleven of us boys ran out onto the field.

* * *

It wasn't the greatest soccer game we ever played. I guess because it was cold and both teams were so nervous about being in the championship, we played like we hadn't been on a soccer field in about three months. Forwards missed easy shots, midfielders tripped over their own feet, and fullbacks always seemed to be in the wrong place at the wrong time. At half time we came back to the bench, leading 1–0 on a penalty kick by Billy. Everyone looked a little sheepish.

Lavelle wasn't thrilled, but he said, "Listen, boys, just keep playing the same game. As long as they play worse than we do, who cares?"

Things shaped up a little during the next half. We scored once and they scored once to make it 2–1. Then, with about a minute left in the game, the other team tried a surprise blitz, sending almost every player on their team except the goalie and fullbacks down the field, overpowering our defense. It looked more like football than soccer, and for a second it seemed as if it might work. I had to jump out of the goal to cut down the angle at which their players could kick the ball, and I was about five feet from their lead man when he booted it as hard as he could. . . .

"David? Hey, David!" Someone was yelling right into my ear.

I opened my eyes. I was lying on my back and the

sky was full of faces—Lavelle's, Chunk's, Billy's, and more. "He's okay," I heard someone yell. Lavelle was smiling. Johnny Jarret leaned in. "That was the best face-save I've ever seen," he said. The ground felt cold under my back and the right side of my face felt numb. Chunk was helping me up, but I felt pretty dizzy. I realized they were walking me off the field and tried to turn back to the goal.

"Forget it, David," Lavelle said. The next thing I knew, I was sitting on the bench and Chunk was in the goal. With one minute left to go our players kept passing the ball around, stalling until time ran out. It worked. The other team didn't even get a shot on Chunk in the goal.

The whistle blew and everyone went crazy. I was still a little groggy as they lifted me up to their shoulders and ran around the bench once. Everybody was congratulating me, but I kept telling them that it was nothing, I'd only used my head. The numbness had changed to stinging, and when we got back to the dressing room, Lavelle had a doctor there who shone a light in my eyes and tested my reflexes. He said I might have a mild concussion and should see a doctor when I got home. In the locker room everybody was celebrating, but when I turned around I saw Johnny Jarret standing next to the Gatorade dispenser with tears in his eyes. He looked up and saw me watching him. A crooked smile appeared on his face. "Well," he said, wiping his nose on his sleeve. "At least we'll never have to drink this stuff again."

"You awake?" Chunk asked.

"Hmm." We were on the bus going home. It was dark out. The only sound was the steady roar of the bus engines as we rolled down Route 17.

"I'm proud of you, partner," he said, tipping up the brim of his cowboy hat. Most of the inside lights were out. I could hardly see Chunk's face.

"How come?"

"It didn't matter for you whether we won today, but you hung in there anyway."

I smiled, although I don't think Chunk could see it. Sure it mattered to me. Just because I wasn't going to be a professional soccer player didn't mean anything. "It mattered, Chunk. Probably more than I want to admit."

"Man, I wish you'd change your mind," Chunk said.

I patted him on the back. "You'll be the first to know if I do, *partner*."

I got home just before dinner. Rena was there. I told everyone we'd won and for a while they looked happy, but by the time we sat down to eat, Rena and my mother looked like they were at a funeral or something.

"What are you guys so grim about?" I asked, checking out the big roast chicken sitting on a platter in the middle of the table, waiting for my father to carve it. On the way home the team had stopped for dinner, but most of us were too excited and tired to eat much. Now I was famished. I nodded toward the bird. "What are you waiting for?" I asked my father.

He scowled and picked up the carving knife.

"Why is your face swollen?" my mother asked.

I told them about the famous face-save. "I'm gonna go see Doctor Brinn tomorrow morning," I said, "just to make sure everything's okay." I didn't tell them about the possibility of a concussion.

My father cleared his throat. "White or dark?"

"Dark, please."

We passed our plates to him and he placed meat on them. Rena's and my eyes met for a moment and then she looked away. My father was staring down at his plate. I couldn't figure out why everyone was so glum. But then it hit me almost as hard as the ball had that afternoon. "Is Howie okay?"

Rena and my mother looked at each other.

"Yes, David," my mother said. "He's all right."

"But . . ." I said, because I knew something was coming.

"Mr. Jamison called yesterday," my mother said. "From West Hill. He said they were transferring Howie to a hospital in Florida. Apparently Howie's condition had stabilized, and they felt he could make the trip. Mr. Jamison said Howie wanted to say good-bye and to tell you he'll write when he gets settled."

I turned to Rena, but she had nothing to say. "What about the house?"

"His father is going to stay up here until they sell it," my dad said.

"You mean he's gone?" I couldn't believe it.

My mother nodded.

No, it couldn't be true. I jumped up and ran outside, but halfway down the driveway I stopped. I didn't really want to go all the way to Howie's to find out. It was cold, but I stood alone in the dark, trying not to believe what I'd just heard. It made me furious. It wasn't fair. I hadn't gotten a chance to see him again. Behind me the front door opened and Rena came out.

"I can't believe it," I said. "I can't believe he'd go without telling me."

"I'm sure he wanted to, David," Rena said. "He cared about you so much."

"Then why didn't he tell me?" I yelled. "He must have known when we were there on Friday."

"Maybe he didn't, David," Rena said. "I heard the hospital didn't want him to leave, but his mother insisted. They had to let him go."

"Oh, bull." I was so mad I couldn't think.

It was too cold for Rena so we went back inside and sat down again. My father had been talking to my mother about something and he turned to me. "If you want to fly down there and see him, we'll pay for it."

"Thanks, Dad."

I guess my mother sensed that Rena and I wanted to be alone and she got my father out of the dining room. Rena lit a cigarette and for a while we both sat, looking across the table at each other.

"Do you think you'll go see him?" she asked.

"Sure."

"I'd like to go too," she said.

"Yeah." Each time I thought of Howie I felt empty inside, like something had been taken away from me. Rena reached across the table and put her hand over mine. She must have felt it too. I guess we both knew we'd been through something that had changed us.

"Don't be angry, David," she said.

She was right. You can't really get angry about things that happen for no reason. It was no one's fault that Howie got sick, and you couldn't really blame Mrs. Jamison for wanting to go back south. Now Howie was gone. Sometimes things just happen. The toughest part is learning to accept that.

AFTERWORD

My father sold the Jamisons' house just after Christmas. Before Mr. Jamison left I went over to see him and he said Howie was still pretty sick. They hadn't been able to get him back into remission with chemotherapy and they were trying to decide what to try next. Mr. Jamison seemed sad, so I didn't ask him anything more, I just helped him load some cabinets into the station wagon. Then he rolled down the driveway and waved good-bye. About a week later a new family moved in.

Over the next couple of months I wrote to Howie three times.

He never wrote back.

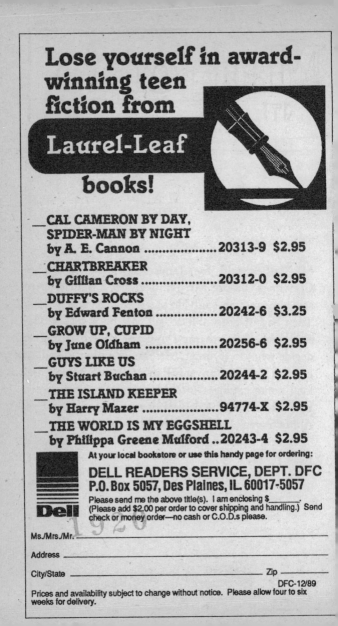